THE SAINT STEPS IN

He skidded around the upturned table and darted through the hall in pursuit. Morgen was out of sight when the Saint got outside and Simon's brain was working like a comptometer now ... Morgen—car keys—a car—the road ... Simon gave a second to clear mechanical thought, and started down the path towards the house. Then he swerved off through a thin space in the shrubbery to try and head off Morgen's retreat.

Something solid but soft intercepted his feet. He spilled forward and sprawled headlong onto the uncut grass.

Then he saw what had tripped him.

It was a body which had been plainly exposed by the encounter. Until recently it had been inhabited by the late Mr. Sylvester Angert.

Other Saint titles published by Charter Books:

THE SAINT

THE SAINT STEPS IN

LESLIE CHARTERIS

CHARTER
NEW YORK

A DIVISION OF CHARTER COMMUNICATIONS INC.
A GROSSET & DUNLAP COMPANY

THE SAINT STEPS IN

Published by arrangement with Doubleday & Company, Inc.

Charter Books
A Division of Charter Communications Inc.
A Grosset & Dunlap Company
360 Park Avenue South
New York, New York   10010

First Charter edition published May 1980

THE SAINT STEPS IN

1.

How Simon Templar dined in Washington, and Sylvester Angert spoke of his Nervousness.

She was young and slender, and she had smiling brown eyes and hair the color of old mahogany. With a lithe grace, she squeezed in beside Simon Templar at the small table in the cocktail room of the Shoreham and said, "You're the Saint."

Simon smiled back, because she was easy to smile at; but not all of the smile went into his very clear blue eyes that always had a faint glint of mockery away behind them, like an amused spectator sitting far back in a respectful audience.

He said: "Am I?"

"I recognised you," she said.

He sighed. The days of happy anonymity that once upon a time had made his lawless career relatively simple seemed suddenly as far away as his last diapers. Not that even today he was as fatefully recognisable as Clark Gable: there were still several million people on earth to whom his face, if not his

1

name, would have meant nothing at all: but he was recognised often enough for it to be what he sometimes called an occupational hazzard.

"I'm afraid there's no prize," he said. "There isn't even a reward out at the moment, so far as I know."

It hadn't always been that way. There had been a time, actually not so very long ago, when half the police departments of the world carried a dossier on the Saint in their active and urgent file, when hardly a month went by without some newspaper headlining a new story on the amazing brigand whom they had christened the Robin Hood of modern crime, and when any stranger accosting the Saint by name would have seen that lean tanned reckless face settle into new lines of piratical impudence, and the long sinewy frame become lazy and supple like the crouch of a jungle cat. Those days might come back again at any time, and probably would; but just now he was almost drearily respectable. The war had changed a lot of things.

"I wanted to talk to you," she said.

"You seem to be making out all right." He looked into his empty glass. "Would you like a drink?"

"Dry Sack."

He managed to get the attention of one of the harried waiters in the crowded place, with an ease that made the performance seem ridiculously simple. He ignored the glowerings of several finger-snapping congressmen, as well as the dark looks of some young lieutenants and ensigns who, because they fought the "Battle of Constitution Avenue" without flinching, thought they deserved a priority on service, Washington's scarcest commodity. Simon ordered the Dry Sack, and had another Peter

Dawson for himself.

"What shall we talk about?" he asked. "I can't tell you the story of my life, because one third of it is unprintable, one third is too incriminating, and the rest of it you wouldn't believe anyhow."

The girl's eyes flashed around the crowded noisy smoky place, and Simon felt the whirring of gears somewhere within him; the gears which instinctively sprang into action when he sensed the possibility of excitement in the offing. And the girl's behavior was just like the beginning of an adventure story.

Her voice was so low that he barely caught her words, when she said: "I was going to ask you to help me."

"Were you?" He looked at her and saw her eyes dart about the cocktail lounge again as if she were momentarily expecting to see someone whose appearance would be decidedly unwelcome. She felt his gaze on her and made an effort to ease the tautness of her face. Her voice was almost conversational when next she spoke.

"I don't know why," she said, "but I'd sort of imagined you in a uniform."

Simon didn't look tired, because he had heard the same dialogue before. He had various answers to it, all of them inaccurate. The plain truth was that most of the things he did best were not done in uniforms—such as the interesing episode which had reached its soul-satisfying finale only twelve hours ago, and which was the reason why he was still in Washington, relaxing over a drink for the first time in seven very strenuous days. But things like that couldn't be talked about for a while.

"I got fired, and my uniform happened to fit the new doorman," he said. He waited until the waiter placed the two drinks on the table. "How do you think I could help you?"

"I suppose you'll think I'm stupid," she said, "but I'm just a little bit frightened."

The slight lift of his right eyebrow was noncommittal.

"Sometimes it's stupid not to be frightened," he said. "It all depends. Excuse the platitudes, but I just want to find out what you mean."

"Do you think anything could happen to anyone in Washington?"

"Anything," said the Saint with conviction, "could happen to anyone in Washington. And most of the time it does. That's why so many people here have ulcers."

"Could anyone be killed here?"

He shrugged.

"There was a man named Stavisky," he offered, "but of course that was officially labeled a suicide. But I could imagine somebody being killed here. Is that the proposition, and whom do you want bumped off?"

She turned the stem of her glass between her fingers, her head bent, not looking at him.

"I'm sorry," she said. "I didn't think you'd be like that."

"I'm sorry too," he said coolly. "But after all, you make the most unusual openings. I only read about these things in magazines. You seem to know something about me. I don't know anything about you, except that I'd rather look at you than a fat senator. Let's begin with the introduction. I don't even know your name."

"Madeline Gray."

"It's a nice name. Should it ring bells?"

"No."

"You aren't working for a newspaper, by any chance?"

"No."

"And you're not a particularly unsophisticated Mata Hari?"

"I—no, of course not."

"You just have an academic interest in whether I think it would be practical to ease a guy off in this village."

"It isn't exactly academic," she said.

He took a cigarette from the pack in front of him on the table.

"I'm sorry, again," he said. "But you sounded so very cheerful and chatty about it—"

"Cheerful and chatty," she interrupted as the tautness returned to her face, "because I don't want anyone who's watching me to know everything I'm talking to you about. I thought you'd be quick enough to get that. And I didn't have in mind any guy who might be eased off, as you put it."

The Saint put a match to his cigarette. Everything inside him was suddenly very quiet and still, like the stillness after the stopping of a clock which had never been noticed until after it left an abrupt intensity of silence.

"Meaning yourself?" he asked easily.

She was spilling things out of her handbag, searching for a lipstick. She found it. The same movement of her hand that picked it up slid a piece of paper out of the junk pile in his direction. Shoulder to shoulder with her as he was, it lay right under his eyes.

In crudely blocked capitals, it said:

DON'T TRY TO SEE IMBERLINE

"I never wanted to see him," said the Saint.

"You don't have to. But I've got an appointment with him at eight o'clock."

"Just who is Imberline?"

"He's in the WPB."

The name began to sound faintly familiar; although Simon Templar had very little more general knowledge of the multitudinous personnel of the various Washington bureaus than any average citizen.

He said: "Hasn't he heard about making the world safe for the forty-hour week?"

"Maybe not."

"And somebody doesn't want you to put him wise."

"I don't know, exactly. All I know is that the note you're looking at was tossed into my lap about twenty minutes ago."

Simon glanced at the paper again. It was wrinkled and crumpled as it should have been, if it had been made into a ball, as the girl implied. He said: "You didn't see where it came from?"

"Of course not."

He admitted that. It could easily have been done. And just as readily he admitted the cold spectral fingers that slid caressingly up his spine. It was right and inevitable, it always had been, that adventure should overtake him like that, just as naturally and just as automatically, as soon as he was "at liberty" again. But when it was too easy and too automatic, also, it could have other angles . . . He was precisely as relaxed and receptive as a seasoned guerilla entering a peaceful valley.

"As a matter of interest," he murmured, "is this the first you've heard about this conspiracy to keep Imberline away from your dazzling beauty?"

"Oh, no," she said. She had regained her composure now and her voice was almost bland. "I had a phone call this morning that was much more explicit. In fact, the man said that if I wanted to live to be a grandmother I'd better start working at it now—and he meant by going home and staying there."

"It sounds like rather a dull method," said the Saint.

"That's why I spoke to you," she said.

The turn of his lips was frankly humorous.

"As a potential grandfather?"

"Because I thought you might be able to get me to see Imberline in one piece."

Simon turned in his chair and looked around the room.

He saw an average section of Official Washington at cocktail time—senators, representatives, bureaucrats, brass hats, men with strings to pull and men with things to see. Out of the babble of conversation, official secrets reverberated through the air in deafening sotto voces that would have gladdened the hearts of a whole army of fifth columnists and spies, and probably did. But all of them shared the sleek solid look of men in authority and security, bravely bearing up under the worry of wondering where their next hundred grand was coming from. None of them had the traditional appearance of men who could spend their spare time carving pretty girls into small sections.

The dialogue would have sounded perfect in a vacuum; but somehow, from where the Saint sat, none of it sounded right. He turned back to Madeline Gray.

"This may sound a bit out of line," he remarked, "but I like to know things in advance. You don't happen to have a heart interest in this Imberline that his spouse or current girl friend might object to?''

She shook her head decisively.

"Heavens, no!"

"Then what do you have to see him about?" he asked, and tried not to seem perfunctory.

"I don't know whether I should tell you that."

The Saint was still very patient. And then he began to laugh inside, it was still fun, and she was really interesting to look at, and after all you couldn't have everything.

A round stocky man who must once have been a door-to-door salesman crowded heavily past the table to a vacant seat nearby and began shouting obstreperously at the nearest waiter. Simon eyed him, decided that he was unusually objectionable, and consulted his watch.

"You've still got more than an hour to spare," he said. "Let's have some food and talk it over."

They had food. He ordered lobster Cardinal and a bottle of Chateau Olivier. And they talked about everything else under the sun. It passed the time surprisingly quickly. She was fun to talk to, although nothing was said that either of them would ever remember. He enjoyed it much more than the solitary meal he had expected. And he was almost sorry when they were at their coffee, and for the sake of the record he had to call a showdown.

He said: "Darling, I've enjoyed every minute of this, and I'll forgive you anything, but if you really wanted me to help you it must have occurred to you that I'd want to have some idea what I was helping. So let's finish the story about Imberline and the mysterious tosser of notes. Since you've told me that Romance hasn't reared its lovely head, that you're not a newspaper gal nor a spy, I'm a bit at a loss."

Her dark eyes studied him quietly for several seconds.

Then she searched through her purse again.

"A filing system," Simon murmured, "would be indicated."

The girl's hand came up with something about six inches long, like a thick piece of tape, and a sort of shiny pale translucent orange in color. She passed it across the table.

Simon took it and fingered it experimentally. It was soft but resistant, tough against the pressure of a thumbnail, flexible and—elastic. He stretched it and snapped it back a couple of times, and then his gaze was cool and estimating on her.

"Rubber?" he asked.

"Synthetic."

His eyebrows hardly moved.

"What kind?"

"Something quite new. It's made mostly of sawdust, vinegar, milk—plus, of course, two or three other important things. But it isn't derived from butadiene."

"That must be a load off its mind," he remarked. "What in the world is butadiene?"

Her unaffected solemnity could have been comic if it had not seemed so completely natural.

"I thought everybody knew that," she said. "Butadiene is something you make out of petroleum, or grain alcohol. It's the base of the buna synthetic rubbers. Of course, that might be a bit technical for you."

"It might," he admitted. He wondered whether she had been taken in by his wide-eyed wonderment or not. He rather thought not.

"The thing that matters," she said, "is that the production of buna is still pretty experimental, and in any case it involves a fairly elaborate and expensive plant. This stuff can be mixed in a bathtub, practically. My father invented it. His name is Calvin Gray. You've probably never heard of him, but he's rated one of the top research chemists in the country."

"And you're here to get Imberline interested in this—to get his WPB sanction?"

She nodded.

"You make it sound frightfully easy. But it hasn't been so far . . . My father started working on this idea years ago, but then natural rubber was so cheap that it didn't seem worth going on with. When the war started and the Japs began moving in on Thailand, he saw what was coming and started working again."

"He must have hundreds of people rooting for him."

"Is that what you think? After he published his first results, his laboratory was burned out once, and blown up twice. Accidents, of course. But he knows, and I know, that they were accidents that had been—arranged. And then, when he had his process perfected, and he came here to try to give it to the Government—you should have seen the run-around they gave him."

"I can imagine it."

"Of course, part of the brush-off he got here might have been his fault. He's quite an individualist, and he hasn't read those books about winning friends and influencing people. At the same time, pardoxically, he's rather easily discouraged. He ended up by damning everybody and going home."

"And so?"

"I came back here for him."

Simon handed the sample back to her with a tinge of regret. It was a lovely performance, and he didn't believe a word of it. He wished that some day some impressionable and personable young piece of loveliness would have the outrageous honesty to come up to him and simply say "I think you're marvelous and I'd give anything to see you in action", without trying to feed him an inferior plot to work on. He felt really sorry about it, because she seemed like nice people and he could have liked her.

"If you think you're on the spot, you ought to talk to the FBI," he said. "Or if you're just getting the old runaround, squawk to one of the papers. If you pick the right one, they'll pour their hearts into a story like that."

She stood up so suddenly that some of his coffee spilled in the saucer. She looked rather fine doing that, and the waste of it hurt him.

"I'm sorry," she said huskily. "It was a silly idea, wasn't it? But it was nice to have dinner with you, just the same."

He sat there quite sympathetically while she walked away.

The dining room seemed unusually dull after she had disappeared. Perhaps, he thought, he had been rather uncouthly hasty. After all, he had been enjoying himself. He could have gone along with the gag.

But then, life was so short, and there were so many important things.

He was sitting there, pondering over the more important things, when a group of men bore down on him, crowding their way through the too-narrow aisles between the tables. In the van of the group was a large person with a domineering air, and Simon knew that he was almost certain to be jostled, as he had been jostled in the cocktail lounge.

He was getting tired of being bumped and shoved by individuals who seemed to get the idea that the "DC" after Washington meant "disregard courtesy". He prepared himself for the inevitable encounter.

The big man did not disappoint him. Simon felt the pressure on the back of his chair, and a coat sleeve ruffled the hair on the back of his head. He shoved back his chair quickly and beamed inwardly as he heard the involuntary "oof" that the big man gave as the chairback dug into his stomach. Templar stretched his lean length upright and turned to the man he had effectively body-checked with his chair.

"Terribly sorry," he said very politely.

The big man looked at him. He had the crimson-mottled face of a person who enjoyed good food, good liquor, and good cigars, and had had too many of each. His little eyes regarded Simon speculatively for a moment, and there might have been a flare behind them, or there might not have been, before he wreathed his face in a beaming smile.

"It's all right," he said. "Accidents will happen, you know."

"Yes, indeed," Simon murmured.

The others in the party were waiting respectfully, almost reverently, for the big man to proceed. The man whom Simon had prodded with the chair gave the Saint another enigmatic glance and then turned away. His disciples followed.

"But Mr. Imberline," one of them cried in a

voice that approached a wail. "Think of the inconvenience that this program will mean to certain parties."

"As the fellow says," announced the prow of the group, majestically. "This is war, and it's up to every one of us to put our shoulders to the wheel. Waste not, want not, is my motto, and this is a case of too many cooks spoiling the broth."

"Incredible," the Saint told himself, gazing after the group as it barged its way to the long table that had been reserved at the further end of the room. "That must be the great Imberline himself."

He put a cigarette between his lips, and felt in his coat pocket for a match.

He didn't find the match, but his fingers encountered something else that he knew at once didn't belong there. It was a folded piece of paper which he knew quite certainly he had never put in that pocket. He took it out and opened it.

It was the same clumsy style of block capitals that he had seen very recently, and it said:

MIND YOUR OWN BUSINESS

He had a curious feeling in looking at it, like walking out of a rowdy stifling honky-tonk into a silent snow night. Because all the time they had been in the cocktail lounge, Madeline Gray had been on his left, and he had been half turned towards her, so that his right-hand pocket was almost against the table, and it was impossible that she could have put that paper into his pocket while they were there. And, aside from the fact that he had been surrounded by Imberline satellites a few seconds earlier, there had definitely been no chance since . . .

2

The doorman said: "Yes, she went that way. She was walking." He put away the dollar bill that Simon handed him, and added: "She asked me the way to Scott Circle."

Simon turned back into the lobby and found a telephone booth. The directory gave him the address of Frank Imberline. It was one of the low numbers on Scott Circle.

Simon Templar frowned thoughtfully.

From the address, it was evident that Mr. Imberline might indeed be a gentleman of some importance, for Scott Circle is the center of one of the best residential sections of Washington, and the list of householders there reads like a snob hostess's dream.

Madeline Gray had told him that she had an appointment with Imberline at eight. He checked his strap watch and saw that it was close to eight now. Still, Imberline—or at least *an* Imberline had just entered the hotel dining room, obviously bent on food. For a fairly prominent bureaucrat to ignore an appointment was not unheard of in Washington, and that might be the answer. Or Frank Imberline might have a brother or a cousin or a namesake who possessed some Government job and its accompanying entourage.

Still . . . Simon wished that he had questioned Madeline about the appointment, and how she had arranged it. For a Government official to arrange an appointment at his home, in the evening, sounded a little strange.

He left the hotel again and acquired a taxi by the subtle expedient of paying an extortionate bribe to a driver who maintained that he was waiting for a customer who had just stepped into the hotel for a moment. With the taxi in motion, Simon sat forward and watched the road all the time with an accelerating impatience that turned into an odd feeling of emptiness as he began to realize that the time was approaching and passing when they should have overtaken the girl. Unless she had taken a different route, or picked up a taxi on the way, or . . .

Or.

Then they were entering Scott Circle, and stopping at the number he had given the driver. He didn't see another taxi at the door, or anywhere in the vicinity.

He got out and paid his fare. The front of the house seemed very dark, except for a light shining through the transom above the door. That was explainable, he told himself, if this really was a romantic tryst, if there was another Imberline besides the one in the hotel dining room, but it seemed to the Saint to be an odd set of circumstances under which a bureaucrat would carry on a conference concerning synthetic rubber.

To the Saint, direct action was always better than dim speculation. He rang the bell.

The butler said: "No, suh, Mr. Imberline ain't to home."

"He is to me," said the Saint cheerfully. "I've got an appointment with him. The name is Gray."

"Ah'm sorry, suh, but Mr. Imberline ain't here. He ain't been back since he left this mawnin', an' he told the cook he was eatin' out."

Simon pursed his lips wryly.

"I guess he forgot his appointment," he said. "I guess, being such a busy man, he forgets a lot of them."

"No suh!" said the butler loyally. "Not Mr. Im-

berline, suh! He makes a date to be somewhere an'
he gits there. Mebbe you got the wrong evenin',
suh. Mebbe it's tomorrer you's supposed to have
your 'pointment."

"Perhaps," the Saint said easily. "I may have
mixed up my times. Tell me, did a young lady
named Gray call here this evening? I rather expected to meet her here."

The woolly white head moved negatively.

"Ain't nobody called here, suh," the butler said.

"Then I must have the dates mixed up."

He turned away from the door, saying things silently to himself. He addressed himself with a sear-
ing minuteness of detail which would almost certainly have been a cue for mayhem if it had been
done by anybody else.

There was still no other cab in sight.

He turned south on 23rd Street, and he had
reached the intersection of Q Street before he
began to wonder where he was going or what good
it was likely to do. He paused uncertainly on the
corner, looking towards the bridge over Rock Creek
Park. A dozen alternatives chased through his mind,
and so many of them must be wrong and so few of
them offered anything to pin much to.

And then he saw her coming around the curve of
the bridge, walking with her young steady stride,
and everything he had imagined seemed foolish
again. For about five or six seconds.

A car came crawling up from behind her, passed
her, stopped, and backed up into an alley that
branched diagonally off from the north side of the
street. He had instinctively stood still and merged
himself into the shadow of a tree when he saw her,
so the two men who came out of the alley a moment
later must have thought the block was deserted ex-

cept for themselves and the girl. They wore hand-kerchiefs tied over the lower part of their faces, and they closed in on her, one on each side, very professionally, and he was too far away to hear whatever they said, but he saw them turn her into the alley as he started running soundlessly towards them.

He came up on them in such a swift catlike silence that it must have seemed to all of them as if a shadow materialised before their eyes.

"Hullo, Madeline," he drawled. "I was afraid I'd missed you, darling."

Her face looked pale and vague in the gloom.

The masked man on her left spoke in muffled accents. He was tall and wide-shouldered, and he seemed to be of the type that never lost a fist fight when he was a schoolboy.

"Better stay out of this, bud, if you don't want to get into trouble."

His voice was a deep hollow rasp, behind the mask. He looked like a man who could provide trouble or cope with it. The man on the other side had much the same air. He weighed a little more, but he was inches shorter and carried it chunkily.

"I like trouble," Simon said breezily. "What kind have you got?"

"FBI trouble," said the tall man flatly. "This girl's—uh—being detained for questioning. Run along."

"Detained?" asked the Saint. "Just why?"

"Beat it," growled the chunky one. "Or we might think of taking you along with us."

"You," said the Saint calmly, "are the first FBI operatives I've ever met who wore handkerchiefs over your noses and so far forgot their polish that they'd say anything like 'beat it', or call anybody 'bud'. If you're posing as G-men, you're making a horrible mess of it. So, if you show your credentials, I'll be happy to go along with the young lady. But I don't think you will, or can."

He was ready for the swing the tall man launched at him, and he swayed back just the essential six inches and let the wind of it fan his chin. Then he shifted his weight forwards again and stepped in with his right forearm pistoning at waist level. The jar of the contact ran all the way up to his shoulders. The tall man grunted and leaned over from the middle and the Saint's left ripped up in a short smash to the mufflered jaw that would have dropped the average citizen in his tracks. The tall man was somewhat tougher than the average. He went pedaling back in a slightly ludicrous race with his own center of gravity, but he still had nothing but his feet on the ground when a large part of his companion's weight descended on the Saint's neck and shoulders.

Simon's eyes were blurred for an instant in a pyrotechnic burst of lights, and his knees began to bend; then he got his hands locked behind the chunky man's head, and let his knees sag even lower before he heaved up again. The chunky man came somersaulting over his shoulder and hit the ground with a thud that a deaf man could have felt several feet away. He rolled over in a wild flurry and wound his arms around the Saint's shins, binding Simon's legs together from ankle to knee.

In a clutch like that, Simon knew that he had no more chance of staying upright than an inverted pyramid. He tried to come down as vertically as possible, so as to stay on top of the chunky man, trying to land on him with his weight on his knees and aiming a downward left at him at the same time.

Neither of those schemes connected. Simon afterwards had a dim impression of running feet, of Madeline Gray crying out something incoherent; then a very considerable weight hit him in the middle and sent him spinning.

Half winded, he grappled blindly for a hold while the man who had tackled him swarmed over him with the same intention. He had had very little leisure for thinking, and so it was a moment or two before he realised that this was not the comeback of the tall bony partner. This man's outlines and architecture were different again. And then even before Simon could puzzle any more about it the girl was clawing at his antagonist, beating ineffectually on his broad back with her fists; but it was enough of an interruption to nullify the Saint's temporary disadvantage, and he got first a knee into the man's stomach, and then one foot in what was more of a shove than a kick, and then he was free and up again and looking swiftly around to see who had to be next.

He was just in time to catch a glimpse of the chunky man's rear elevation as it fell into the parked car a few yards away. The tall bony one had already disappeared, and presumably he was at the wheel, for the engine roared up even before the door slammed, and the car leapt away with a grind of spinning tires that would have made any normal war-time motorist wince. It screamed out of the alley as Simon turned again to look for the third member of the opposition.

The third member was holding one hand over his diaphragm and making jerky little bows over it, and saying in a painful and puzzled voice: "My God . . . You're Miss Gray, aren't you?"

As Simon stepped towards him he said: "Damn,

I'm sorry. I must have picked the wrong side. I was just driving by—"

"You've got a car?" Simon snapped.

"Yes. I just got out—"

Simon caught the girl's hand and raced to the street. There was a convertible parked just beyond the alley, but it was headed in the opposite direction from the way the escaping car had turned. And the other car itself was already out of sight.

The Saint shrugged and searched for a consoling cigarette.

"I'm really terribly sorry." The other man came up with them, still holding his stomach and trying to straighten himself. "I just saw the fight going on, and it looked as if someone was in trouble, and naturally I thought the man on the ground was the victim. Until Miss Gray started beating me up . . . I'm afraid I helped them get away."

"You know each other, do you?" asked the Saint. She was staring puzzledly.

"I've seen you somewhere, but—"

"Walter Devan," said the man. "It was in Mr. Quennel's office. You were with your father."

Simon put a match to his cigarette. With the help of that better light, he shared with her a better view of the man's face. It was square-jawed and powerful, with the craggy leathery look of a prizefighter.

"Oh yes!" She turned to the Saint. "Mr. Devan —Mr. Templar."

Simon put out his hand.

"That's quite a flying tackle you have," he said, and Devan grinned.

"It should be—I played professional football when I was a lot younger. You're a pretty good kicker yourself."

"We are a lot of wasted talent," said the Saint.

"Perhaps it's all for the best," Devan said. "Anyway, we got rid of those hoodlums, and some of them can be very ugly. There have been a lot of hold-ups and housebreakings around here lately. The bad boys hide in the park and come out after dark."

Simon thought of mentioning the fact that these particular bad boys had had a car, but decided that for the moment the point wasn't worth making. Before the girl could make any comment, he said: "Maybe you wouldn't mind giving us a lift out of the danger zone."

"Be glad to. Anywhere."

They got in, Madeline Gray in the middle, and Simon looked at her as Devan pressed the starter, and said: "I think we ought to go back to the Shoreham and have another drink."

"But I've still got to see Mr. Imberline."

"Mr. Imberline isn't home, darling. I was there first. I missed you on the way. Then I started back to look for you."

"But I had an appointment."

"You mean Frank Imberline?" Devan put in.
She said: "Yes."

"Mr. Templar's right. He's not home. I happen to know that because Mr. Quennel's been trying to get in touch with him himself."

"Just how did you get this appointment?" Simon asked.

"I'd been trying to see him at his office," she said, "but I hadn't gotten anywhere. I'd left my name and address, and they were supposed to get in touch with me. Then I got a phone call this afternoon to go to his house."

"Someone was pulling your leg," said the Saint quietly.

She looked at him with wide startled eyes.

Simon's arm lay along the back of the seat behind her. His left hand moved on her shoulder with a firm significant pressure. Until he knew much more about everything, now, he was in no hurry to talk before any strangers.

Especially this man who called himself Walter Devan.

Because, unless he was very much mistaken, Devan had been the round stocky man who had jostled him in the Shoreham cocktail lounge. And the eyes of the taller of the two self-asserted FBI agents looked very much like those of one of the group that had followed Frank Imberline into the dining room later—when he had received his second jostling.

3

Devan seemed quite unconscious of any suppression. He said conversationally: "By the way, Miss Gray, how is your father getting on with his new synthetic process?"

"The process is fine," she said frankly, "but we're still trying to put it over."

Devan shook his head sympathetically.

"These things take a lot of time. Imberline may be able to help you," he said. "It's too bad our company couldn't do anything about it." He turned towards Simon and added in explanation: "Mr. Gray has a very promising angle on the synthetic rubber problem. He brought it to Mr. Quennel, but unfortunately it wasn't in our line."

"I suppose," said the Saint, "I should know—but what exactly is your line?"

"Quennel Chemical Corporation. Quenco Products. You've probably seen the name somewhere.

It's rather a well-known name."

His voice reflected quiet pride. Yes, Simon had seen the name, right enough. When he had first heard it mentioned it had sounded familiar, but he hadn't been able to place it.

"What do you think of Mr. Gray's formula?" he asked.

"I'm afraid I'm not a chemist," Devan said apologetically. "I'm just the personnel manager. It sounds very hopeful, from what I've heard of it. But Quennel already has an enormous contract with the Government for buna, and we've already invested more than two million dollars in a plant that's being built now, so our hands are tied. That's probably our bad luck."

The Saint dragged at his cigarette thoughtfully.

"But if Mr. Gray's invention is successful and put into production, it would mean his method would be in competition with yours, wouldn't it?" he asked.

Devan gave a short laugh.

"I suppose it would be, theoretically," he admitted. "But with the world howling for rubber, all the rubber it can get, it would be hard to call it competition. Rather, it would be like two firms turning out different makes of life preservers—there'd be no pick and choose involved when a drowning man was being thrown one."

The Saint finished his cigarette in silence, with thoughtful leisuredness. There was, after all, some justice in the world. That violent and accidental meeting had its own unexpected compensation for the loss of two possibly unimportant muscle men. If he still needed it, he had the clinching confirmation that the story which had sounded so preposterous was true—that after all Madeline Gray was not just

a silly sensation-hunter and celebrity-nuisance, but
that the invention of Calvin Gray might indeed be
one of those rare fuses from which could explode a
fiesta of fun and games of the real original vintage
that he loved. He felt a little foolish now for some of
his facile incredulity; and yet, glancing again at the
profile of the girl beside him, he couldn't feel very
deeply sorry. It was worth much more than a little
transient egotism for her to be real . . .

They were at the Shoreham, and Walter Devan
said: "I hope I'll see you again."

"I'm staying here," said the Saint.

"So am I," said the girl.

The Saint looked at her and began to raise a
quizzical eyebrow at himself, and she laughed and
said: "I suppose I'd do better if I could act more like
a starving inventor's daughter, but the trouble is we
just aren't starving yet."

He looked at the Scottish tweed suit that covered
her perfection, at the hat that just missed ridicu-
lousness, and silently estimated their cost. No,
Madeline Gray looked as though she was far removed from starvation.

"Let me know if I can help," said Devan. "I
might be able to do something for you. Maybe Mr.
Quennel can reach Imberline and fix some kind of a
conference. I'm at the Raleigh if you should want to
reach me for any reason."

He drove off after a brief word to Templar. Simon gazed after the ruby tail light for a moment,
and then took the girl's arm, steering her into the
lobby. She started to turn towards the cocktail
lounge, but he guided her towards the elevators.

"Let's go to my apartment," he said. "Funny
things seem to happen in cocktail lounges and dining rooms."

He felt her eyes switch to him quickly, but his face was as impersonal as the way he had spoken. She stepped into the elevator without speaking, and was silent until they were in his living room.

At a time when a closet and a blanket could be rented in Washington as a fairly luxurious bedroom, it was still only natural that Simon Templar should have achieved a commodious suite all to himself. He had a profound appreciation of the more expensive refinements of living when he could get them, and he had ways of getting them that would have been quite incomprehensible to less enterprising men. He took off his coat and went to a side table to pour Peter Dawson into two tall glasses, and added ice from a thermos bucket.

"Now," she said, "will you tell me exactly what you mean by funny things happen in cocktail lounges and dining rooms?"

He gave her one of the drinks he had mixed, and then with his freed hand he showed her the note he had found in his pocket.

"I found it just after you'd left," he explained. "That's why I went after you. I'm sorry. I take it all back. I was stupid enough to think you were stupid. I've tried to make up for a little. Now can we start again?"

She smiled at him with a straightforward friendliness that he should have been able to expect. Yet it was still good to see it.

"Of course," she said. "Will you really help me with Imberline when I get in touch with him?"

He sipped his drink casually and looked at her over the rim of his glass. When he took down the drink, he asked:

"Have you ever met this phantom Imberline who everybody seems to be trying to get in touch with?"

She nodded.

"I've seen him a couple of times," she said briefly.

"What's he like, and what does he do?"

She waved her hands expressively.

"He's—oh, he's a Babbitty sort of person, nice but dull and I suspect not too brilliant. Honest, politically ambitious perhaps, a joiner, likes to make friends—"

"Just what is his position?" asked the Saint.

"He's with the WPB, as I told you. A dollar-a-year man in the synthetic rubber branch. Not the biggest man in that branch, but still fairly important. He has quite a bit of say about what money is going to be spent for the development of which processes."

The ice in Simon's glass tinkled as he drank again.

"And what did he do before he became a dollar-a-year man?" he asked.

Her eyes widened a trifle as she gazed back at him.

"Surely, you must have heard of Frank Imberline!" she exclaimed. "Imberline, of Consolidated Rubber. Of course, it was his father who built up the rubber combine, but at least this Imberline hasn't done anything to weaken that combine. There are hints, rumors—"

She broke off abruptly and gnawed her lip.

"Go on," said Simon pleasantly. "I'm interested in the saga of The Imberline."

She moved her hands again.

"Oh, it's just rubber trade talk," she said. "Something you couldn't possibly be interested in."

"Suppose I hear it and decide for myself."

"Well—Father doesn't like Imberline, and he

may be prejudiced—probably is. But he maintains Imberline is nothing more than a straw man for a syndicate of unscrupulous men who wangled his WPB appointment in order to further their own ends. I told you that Father's an individualist. I suppose that's a nice way of hinting that he's a near-eccentric. Some inventors are. He's frightfully bitter against the people in Washington who gave him the runaround, and he insists that certain interests are trying to smother his process in order to build up their own business during the war and, more selfishly, after the war."

"And your father, I take it, has only the good of the people at heart."

She looked down at her drink and he spoke swiftly.

"I'm sorry," he said. "A few days of Washington and I find myself afflicted with cynicism."

"It's all right," she said in a low voice. "It was a logical question, after all."

She raised her eyes to his and met them squarely.

"Yes," she said stoutly. "He does have the good of the people at heart. He offered his invention to the Government, free and clear, but his offer never got to the men he wanted to give it to. Instead, he was interviewed by strangers whom he didn't like or trust. When he refused to give them his formula, when he insisted on being taken to the top man, the mysterious accidents began to happen."

"Does Imberline know of all this?"

She shrugged.

"Who knows? I've told you that he's not exactly the heavy intellectual. It might be that he's of the popular conviction that all inventors are pathological specimens who just want to waste his time. Heaven knows he must meet plenty of that type, too. Or it might be that somebody in his office does work for some other interests, as Father insists, and never lets him see anything or anybody they don't want him to see."

She leaned forward eagerly.

"But I'm sure that if I could get to him, I could make him listen, get him interested." She colored slightly. "Frank Imberline, you see, is one of those I'm-old-enough-to-be-your-father persons. I—I think he'll at least give me a hearing."

Simon eyed the girl soberly. Her face blazed suddenly.

"I know what you're thinking," she said. "But I can put up with that if it would help Father and— yes—help the war effort. It sounds corny, I know, but I really mean it."

Her eyes were beseeching.

"Couldn't you help me to see Imberline?" she pleaded.

He gazed at her soberly. She was not stupid in the way he had thought, but it appeared that there were certain of the facts of life that had not yet completely entered her awareness.

"Of course I will," he said kindly. "But it might take some time to get an audience with the pontiff. I'm not so well up in the routines for getting into the inner sanctum of a Washington panjandrum . . ."

The Saint had a faculty of hearing things without listening for them, and of correlating them with the instantaneous efficiency of a sorting machine, so that they were sharply classified in his mind almost before the mechanical part of his sense of hearing had finished processing them.

This particular sound was no more than the shyest ghost of a tap. But it told him, quite simply and clearly, that something had touched the door behind him.

He moved towards it on soundless feet, while his voice went on without the slightest change of pace or inflection.

". . . I believe if you take a folding cot and a camp stove and park in his outer office for a few days you can sometimes get in a word with his secretary's secretary's secretary . . ."

Simon's hand touched the doorknob and whipped the door open in one movement of lightning suddenness. And with another movement that followed the first with the precision of a reciprocating engine, he shot out another hand to grasp the collar of the man who crouched outside with an article like a small old-fashioned ear-trumpet at his ear.

"Come in, chum," he said cordially. "Come in and introduce yourself. Are you the house detective, or were you just feeling lonely?"

4

The eavesdropper found himself whirled into the room, clutching wildly at the air in a vain effort to regain his balance. Before he could recover himself, one of his arms was hauled up painfully behind his back, and he found himself helpless.

"Don't scream, darling," Simon said to the girl. "It's just a surprise visit from somebody who wanted to make certain he wasn't intruding before he knocked."

His free hand moved swiftly over his captive's clothes, but discovered no gun. Simon twisted the eavesdropper around and stared into his face. Then he relaxed his hold on the stranger's arm. The man cautiously stretched the twisted member and began rubbing it, half whimpering as he did.

"Know him?" asked the Saint of the girl.

Wordlessly, Madeline Gray shook her head.

"Not exactly the type," Simon remarked, cocking his head on one side. "He looks more like the typical bookkeeper who's due to get pensioned off with a nice gold watch for fifty years of uninterrupted service, and never a vacation or a day off for sickness."

The little man continued rubbing his arm, squeaking. He looked something like a careworn mouse in ill-fitting clothes, with shoe-button eyes and two rodent teeth that protruded over his lower lip. As the pain in his arm subsided, he worked hard to present a picture of outraged innocence.

"Sir!" he began.

"Even talks like a mouse," observed the Saint coolly.

"I'll have satisfaction for this," said the eavesdropper. "This is—this is scandalous! When a man is attacked in the hallway of a prominent hotel by a hoodlum who practically breaks his arm, it's time—"

"All right, Junior," the Saint said pleasantly. "We can do without all that. Just who are you and who do you work for?"

The little man drew himself up to his full height of about five feet three.

"I might ask you the same question," he retorted. "Who are you that you think you can attack—"

"Look," said the Saint. "I haven't much time, and although I'm usually an exceedingly patient sort of bloke, I'm slightly allergic to people who listen at my door with patent listening gadgets. Who sent you here and what did you expect to find out?"

"My name," squeaked the little man, "is Sylvester Angert. And I was not listening at your door. I was trying to find my own room. I thought this was it. I was about to try my key in the lock when you assaulted me."

"I see," said the Saint thoughtfully. "Of course, you didn't check the number of my room with the number on your key before you—er—prepared to try the lock. And you always have a good reason to listen to what might be going on inside your room before you enter. Is that it?"

The little man's eyes held Simon's firmly for a second and then slid away.

"If you must know," he said, with a spark of defiance, "that's exactly what I do. Listen, I mean. I've done that ever since I had an unpleasant experience in Milwaukee. I walked into my room, and I was held up by two thugs who were waiting for me there. I procured this little instrument to safeguard myself against just that sort of thing."

"Oh, Lord," said the Saint faintly. "Now I've heard everything."

"Believe it or not," said Sylvester Angert, "that's the truth."

"Suppose you show me your key," Simon suggested.

Mr. Angert probed his pockets and came up with the tabbed key and offered it to the Saint. Simon checked the number and frowned thoughtfully. Its last two digits corresponded with the number of Simon's room. Mr. Angert, it appeared, occupied the suite immediately above the Saint's.

Simon returned the key and smiled easily.

"Everything checks beautifully, doesn't it?" he asked. "Suppose you have a seat, Sylvester, and toy with a drink while we talk this over."

Reluctantly the little man took a chair across the room from the door. Simon splashed liquor into a glass and fizzed the soda syphon. He nodded in the direction of the girl.

"I suppose introductions are in order," he said. "Mr. Angert, this is Miss Millie Van Ess. Miss Van Ess, Mr. Angert."

His eyes were bland but they would not have missed the minutest change in Angert's expression, if there had been any reaction to the alias he had inflicted on Madeline Gray. But he saw no reaction at all.

The little man nodded stiffly to the girl and murmured something that might have been "How do you do." He took the glass from Simon and sipped the highball daintily.

Simon's long brown fingers reached for a cigarette.

"Now, Mr. Angert," he said. "I'm sure you'll agree that explanations are in order—on both sides, possibly. Just what is your business, Comrade?"

The liquor seemed to give the little man courage, or perhaps it was the realisation that he was not going to be stretched on a rack—at least not immediately. Over the rim of his glass, he said: "I don't know your name, sir."

"So sorry. It's Templar, Simon Templar."

Angert's voice was quite calm as he said: "I believe I've heard of you. Aren't you the one they call the Saint, or some such name?"

Simon bowed modestly.

"My wife, that's Mrs. Angert, takes a great interest in the crime news in the papers, and I've heard her mention your name. I, personally, don't pay much attention to that sort of thing." He looked up apologetically. "Not," he added, "that I have anything against crime news, but—"

Simon held up a hand.

"No apologies, please," he said. "I much prefer the funnies and the produce market reports, myself. But what do you do, brother, besides not read crime news?"

The little man delved into a vest pocket and brought out a card. Simon read that Sylvester was sales manager of the Choctaw Pipe and Tube Company of Cleveland.

"I'm in Washington, trying to get to see somebody about a subcontract, but, oh dear, I just haven't been able to do *anything!* They all keep sending me from one office to the other and then back to the place I contacted first."

Simon casually slipped the card into his pocket and dragged at his cigarette.

"I take it you make pipes and tubes," he said.

"We did, up until the war," explained Sylvester. "Then we converted to more direct war products. Naturally, I can't explain just what we're turning out now, but it's important. Yessiree, very important, if I may say so."

"I'm sure you may," Simon murmured.

Then he shot his next question in a rapier-like tone that cut away the smug complacency Sylvester seemed to be building up as thoroughly as a sharp knife would rip away cheesecloth.

"Does your plant have anything to do with rubber?" he demanded.

This time Mr. Angert's eyes bounced a bit. He had been prepared for the other questions, but this one had come out of nowhere and there was a split second's interval before he recovered.

"Rubber? Oh no. We're a metal production outfit. No, we have nothing to do with rubber at all."

Simon half turned away to freshen his drink.

"Naturally not," he said. "That was rather a silly question."

Sylvester Angert finished his drink and got out of his chair. He laughed rather uncertainly.

"I'm sorry I was so—so harsh when I first—er—arrived here, but the surprise . . . I guess I do owe you an apology at that. Perhaps we could get together for a drink tomorrow."

"Perhaps," said the Saint noncommittally.

"And now I'd better be getting up to my room. It's getting late and I've had a hard day. Goodnight Miss Van Ess, Mr. Templar."

He ducked his head and scuttled out of the room.

Madeline giggled.

"A funny little man," she said.

"Very. Will you excuse me for a second? I've got a couple of calls to make."

He went into the bedroom, closing the door behind him. He called a local number which was not in any directory, and talked briefly with a man named Hamilton, whom very few people knew. Then he called the desk, and exchanged a few words with information. He returned to the living room, smiling in his satisfaction.

"A funny little man indeed," he said. "There is no such animal as the Choctaw Pipe and Tube Company of Cleveland. And the suite above this is occupied by a senator who's been living there ever since his misguided constituents banded together in a conspiracy to get him out of his home state."

"Then—"

"Oh, he's harmless," the Saint assured her. "I don't think he'll bother us again. It will be somebody very different from little Sylvester who'll probably get the next assignment."

"But who's he working for?"

"The same people, my dear, who seem to be determined that your father's invention is going to blush unseen. I only hope for your sake that hereafter they limit their activities to such things as visits by Sylvester Angert. But I'm afraid they won't."

"What difference does it make?" she protested. "If you'll really help me—and if you're really like any of the things I've read about you—you should be able to wangle an appointment with Imberline in a few days at the outside."

The Saint's fingers combed through his hair. The piratical chiseling of his face looked suddenly quite old in a sardonic and careless way.

"I know, darling," he said. "That isn't the problem. The job that's going to keep me busy is trying to make sure that you and your father are allowed to live that long."

2

How Simon Templar Interviewed Mr. Imberline, and was Interviewed in his Turn.

A change of expression flickered over her face, that started with a half smile and ended with half a frown; but under the half-frown her brown eyes were level and steady.

"Now are you giving me what you thought I was asking for, or do you mean that?"

"Think it out for yourself," he said patiently. "Somebody was interested enough to make your father a present of two explosions and a fire—according to what you told me. Somebody followed you long enough to know you'd been trying to see Imberline. Somebody thought it was worth while calling you and making a phony appointment, and then sending you a threatening note to see how easily you'd scare off. Somebody even thought it was worth while trying another note on me, after they'd seen us talking."

"You don't know how it got into your pocket?"

"No more than you know how yours fell into your lap. But I was bumped into rather heavily on two occasions, so it was on one of those occasions that the note was planted." The face of Walter Devan and the tall man who had been in Imberline's entourage passed through the Saint's memory. "Anyway, since you didn't scare, there was an ambush waiting for you on the way. If you'd taken a cab it doubtless would have been run off the road."

She was neither frightened nor foolish now. She simply watched his face estimatingly.

"What do you think they meant to do?"

"Your guess is as good as mine. Maybe they were just told to rough you up a bit to discourage you. Maybe it was to be a straight kidnapping. Maybe they thought you could be used to keep your father quiet. Or maybe they thought you might be able to tell them his process if they persuaded you enough. By the way, could you?"

She nodded.

"It's very simple, once you know it; and I've been helping Father in his laboratory ever since he started working on it again."

"Then you don't need to ask me questions about what they might have had in mind."

She glanced at her drink.

"It's silly, isn't it? I hadn't thought of it that way."

"You'd better start thinking now. In times like these, anybody who can pour a lot of sawdust, old shoelaces, tomato ketchup, and hair tonic into a bathtub and make rubber is hotter than tobasco. The only thing I can't understand is why the FBI didn't have you both in a fireproof vault long ago."

"I can answer that," she said wearily. "Have you any idea how many new synthetic rubber inventors are pestering people in Washington every day? Only about a dozen."

"But if your father's reputation is as good as you say it is—"

"All sorts of crackpots have some kind of reputation too. And to the average dollar-a-year man, any scientist is liable to be a bit of a crackpot."

"Well, they can test this stuff of yours, can't they?"

"Yes. But that takes a lot of time and red tape. And it wouldn't necessarily prove anything."

"Why not?"

"The specimen might be any other kind of worked-over or reclaimed rubber."

"Surely it could be detected."

"How?"

"Analyse it."

She laughed a little.

"You're not a chemist. Any organic or semi-organic concoction—like this is—is almost impossible to analyse. How can I explain that? Look, for instance, you could grind up the ashes of a human arm, and analyse them, and find a lot of ingredients, but that wouldn't prove whether you'd started with a man or not. That's putting it very clumsily, I know, but—"

"I get the idea."

He lighted a cigarette and tightened his lips on it. These were ramifications that he hadn't had time to think out. But they made sense within the limits of his knowledge.

He went back to the concrete approach that he understood better.

"Has your father patented his formula?"

"No. That would have meant discussing it with

attorneys and petty officials and all kinds of people. And I tell you, it's so simple that if one wrong person knew it, all the wrong people could know it. And after all—we are in the middle of a war."

"He didn't want any commercial protection?"

"I told you that once, and I meant it. He doesn't need money; doesn't want it. Really, we're horribly comfortable. My grandfather bought a gold mine in California for two old mules and a can of corned beef. All Father is trying to do is to give his process to the right people. But he's been soured by his experiences here in Washington, and of course he can't just write a letter or fill out a form, and tell all about it, because then it would be sure to leak out to the wrong people."

"Something seems to have leaked out already," Simon observed.

"Maybe some people have more imagination than others."

"You haven't anyone special in mind?"

She moved her hands helplessly.

"The Nazis?" she suggested. "But I don't know how they'd have heard of it . . . Or the Japs. Or anyone . . ."

"Anyone," said the Saint, "is a fair guess. They don't necessarily have to be clanking around with swastikas embroidered on their underwear and sealed orders from the Gestapo up their sleeves. Anyone who isn't as big-hearted as your father, but who believes in him, might be glad to get hold of this recipe—just for the money. Which would make the field a good bet on any mutuel." He smiled and added: "Even including that human also-ran, Mr. Sylvester Angert—the funny little man."

He put down his glass and strolled around the

room, his hands in his pockets and his eyes crinkled against the smoke of the cigarette slanted between his lips.

It began to look like a nice little situation. The FBI wouldn't have any jurisdiction, unless somebody Higher Up—such as Frank Imberline, perhaps—brought it to Mr. Hoover's attention that the protection of Calvin Gray and his daughter was a matter of national importance. Imberline might do just that, doubtless adding something like: "A stitch in time saves nine." But would he? Would the dollar-a-year man who had been the head of Consolidated Rubber go to any great lengths to protect the life of an inventor of a process which could make synthetic rubber out of old bits of nothing much? Might not Imberline, like too many others in Washington, be looking beyond the end of the war? Walter Devan had said something pat about life preservers, but wasn't it a fact, still, that when the war was over, the old battle might start again; the battle between the old and the war-born new?

Imberline was an unknown quantity, then, which left only the local gendarmerie to appeal to. Simon know nothing at all about them; but even if they were extremely efficient, he surmised that they were also liable to be very busy. He didn't know for how long they would be likely to detach three able-bodied officers for the sole job of providing a full-time personal bodyguard for Madeline Gray. And in any case, they couldn't stay with her if she left the city.

"Where is your father now?" he asked.

"At home—in Connecticut."

"Where?"

"Near Stamford."

The DC police couldn't do anything about that.

And the Stamford cops would be even less likely to have men to spare for an indefinite vigil.

"Maybe you ought to hire some guards from a detective agency," he said. "I gather you could afford it."

She looked him in the eyes.

"Yes. We could afford it."

He had made a reasonable suggestion and she had considered it in the same reasonable way. Even that steady glance of hers didn't accuse him of trying to evade anything. It would have had no right to, anyway, he told himself. It was his own conscience. He didn't owe her anything. He had plenty of other things to think about. There certainly must be some proper legal authority for her to take her troubles to—he just hadn't been able to think what it was. And anyhow, what real basis did he have for deciding that Calvin Gray's invention was practical and important? There were highly trained experts in Government offices who were much more competent to judge such matters than he was.

And just the same he knew that he was still evading, and he felt exasperated with himself.

He asked: "What was your idea when you did see Imberline?"

"Get him to come to the laboratory himself, or send someone who was absolutely reliable. They could watch us make as much rubber as they'd need for their tests, and then they could be sure it was a genuine synthetic."

"But eventually other people would have to be in on it—if it were going to be manufactured in any quantity."

"Father has that all worked out. You could have a dozen different ingredients shipped to the plant and stored in tanks. Three of them would be the vital part of the formula. The other nine would mean nothing. But they'd all be piped down through a mixing room that only one man need go into. The unnecessary ingredients would be destroyed by acids and run down the drain, so that no checkup would be possible. The real formula would be piped from the mixing room direct to the vats. One man could control a whole plant by just working two or three hours a day. I could control one myself. But even if anyone on the outside knew every chemical that was brought in and used, it would taken them years to try out every combination and proportion and treatment until they might hit on the right one."

It was a sound answer. But it had the tinge of being a pat answer, too. As if it had been rehearsed carefully to reply to embarrassing questions.

Or maybe he still had a hangover of his own first skepticism.

He made a decision with characteristic abruptness.

"Suppose," he suggested, "you go to your room. Lock and night-lock the door and don't open it to anyone, except me."

He went to the desk, scrawled a word on a slip of paper, folded it and handed it to her. She looked at it and nodded. He took the paper back and touched a match to it. As the ashes crumbled, they took into nothingness the word he had written, the word he was to say when he called her.

He was taking no chances that Mr. Sylvester Angert's cousin might be looking for his room in the hall outside, complete with a little tube that heard through doors.

"Will you be long?" she asked.

"I hope not. I'll take you to your room, if you don't mind."

"I'd appreciate it."

He escorted her to the elevators, rode up five floors, and saw her safely to her door. He waited until the night latch clicked and then returned to the elevators. He rode to the main lobby and spent a few minutes looking into the dining room. It was virtually deserted—for Washington—and the man he was looking for wasn't there.

Simon left the hotel and bought a taxi driver for the second time that night.

He leaned back on the cracked-leather upholstery and reached for a cigarette.

"Take me to a street that enters into Scott Circle," he directed. "One that hits the circle near the low numbers."

"You got any special number in mind, Chief?"

"Yeah, bud. I got me a number in mind, but just do like I told you, see?"

"Okay, okay. I just wanted to know."

He lit his cigarette, wondering if his tough-guy talk would convince a radio casting director, in a pinch. He decided that it wouldn't. He hadn't used it for quite a while, and he was out of practice. He made a mental note to polish up on it.

The cab drifted to a street corner on the rim of the circle, and the hackman turned.

"How's this, Cap?" he asked.

"This is swell."

He paid off the driver, waited until the cab drove away, and waited a few minutes more to make certain that the cabbie was not too curious. He surveyed the dimmed-out houses on the circle and picked out the mansion which he had already visited once this evening.

There was a light in the downstairs hallway and lights in a second-floor room that must be a bedroom. As he watched, Simon saw a bulky shadow pass the drawn shade. The shadow was of proportions that hardly could have belonged to anyone else but Frank Imberline.

The downstairs light went out. The Saint moved along the sidewalk enough to see a tiny window in the back of the house go on. That meant that the colored butler must be going to bed.

Walking in the deep shadows, Simon Templar made his way to the front door of the house that surely must have been built as an ambassadorial dwelling. He worked on the lock for about a minute with an instrument from his pocket, and it ceased to be an obstruction.

"Now," he told himself, "if there's no burglar alarm, and if there's no bolt, we might get to see Comrade Imberline in person."

There was neither alarm nor bolt. Simon let himself noiselessly into the front hall and closed the door gently behind him. A circular staircase wound its way up toward the second floor, and there was no creak of a loose joist as the Saint made his way aloft. A crack of light under a door told him that Frank Imberline was still awake.

Simon pushed open the door and calmly walked into the great man's bedroom.

Imberline was seated at a desk, scanning a sheaf of papers. He was clad in maroon and gold pajamas that made the Saint blink for a moment. As Simon stepped into the room, the rubber tycoon swung his heavy head in his direction and popped his eyes, the unhealthy ruddiness slowly ebbing from his face.

"Who are you?" he croaked.

"Don't be alarmed, Mr. Imberline," said the Saint soothingly. "I'm not a hold-up man, and I'm not an indignant taxpayer proposing to beat you up."

"Then who the devil are you, and what do you want?"

"My name is Simon Templar, and I just wanted to talk to you."

"How did you get in here?"

"I walked in," said the Saint, "through the front door."

"You broke in!"

Simon shook his head.

"I didn't break anything," he said innocently. "I just used one of my little tricks on the lock. Really, I did no damage at all."

Imberline made gargling noises in his throat.

"This is—this is—"

"I know," said the Saint wearily. "I know, I should have applied for an audience through the usual channels, and filled out half a dozen forms in quintuplicate. But after all there is a war going on —to coin a phrase—and it just occurred to me that this might save us waiting a few months to meet each other."

The red came back into Frank Imberline's square face and he seemed to swell within his gorgeous pajamas.

"I'll have you know," he said, in a half-bellow, "that such high-handed tactics as this—these— must be dealt with by the proper authorities! I will not be intimidated, sir, by any high-handed—"

"You said that before," Simon reminded him politely.

"Well—what in hell do you want?"

"I want to talk to you about a man who has invented a synthetic rubber process. One Calvin Gray."

Imberline drew his heavy brows down over his little eyes.

"What about Calvin Gray?" he demanded.

"I'm interested in Mr. Gray's process," said the Saint, "and I'm wondering why the man can't get a hearing with you."

Imberline waved a pudgy hand in a disdainful gesture.

"A nut, Mr.—er—Templar," he said. "A nut, pure and simple. From what I've heard, he claims he can make rubber out of rhubarb, or something. Impossible, of course. I hope you haven't invested any money in his invention, sir."

"A fool and his money are soon parted," Simon said wisely.

"Yes," Imberline grunted. "Quite so. But this outrageous breaking into a man's house—a man's house is his castle, you know—you really have no excuse for that."

The big man got out of the chair by the desk and stalked over to the bureau. He took a fat cigar from the box on the bureau top and rammed it into his mouth. Simon's eyes were watchful. But Imberline's hand did not move toward the handle of any drawer that might have contained a gun. He marched back across the room and slumped down into a deep easy chair.

"Okay," he said over his cigar. "So you broke in here to talk to me about Gray's invention. I could throw you out or have you arrested, but instead I'll listen to what you have to say."

"Very kind of you," Simon murmured. "A soft answer turneth away stuff."

"What is it you want to know?" Imberline asked bluntly. "I'm a busy man, and every minute counts."

"While time and tide wait for no man."

"Get to the point. Why are you here?"

Simon placed a cigarette between his lips and snapped his lighter. He was aware of Imberline's gimlet eyes watching his every movement. He exhaled a long plume of smoke and sat on the end of the bed.

"Have you ever seen Gray's product?" he asked.

"Once—or maybe twice."

"And what was your opinion?"

If it were possible for the hulking shoulders of Frank Imberline to shrug, they would have.

"It's something that could be synthetic—and it's something that could be made-over rubber, cleverly disguised."

"You investigated it thoroughly, I suppose?"

"I had my staff investigate it. Their report was bad. That man Gray pestered me for weeks, trying to get to see me, and finally gave up. I hear his daughter is in town now, still trying to waste my time."

"You haven't made an appointment with her?"

"Certainly not. There are only so many hours in the day—"

"And so many days in the week—"

"Young man," said Mr. Imberline magisterially, "I am a public servant. I have the most humble respect for the trust which has been placed in me, and my daily responsibility is to make sure that not one hour—not one minute—of my time shall be frittered away on things from which the Community cannot benefit."

"You couldn't by any chance have made an ap-

pointment with her for tonight and forgotten it?"
Simon asked, unawed by that resounding
statement.

Imberline drew his chins together.

"Certainly not! I never forget an appointment.
Punctuality is the politeness of princes—"

"You really ought to have seen her. She's quite
something to look at."

There seemed to be a flicker of interest in the
close-set eyes. Suddenly, the middle-aged lecher
was there for Simon to see. The big man grinned
nauseatingly.

"A nice dish, eh?"

"A very nice dish. But to get back to Gray's invention—you haven't seen it demonstrated yourself, I take it?"

Imberline shook his head.

"No. I'm a busy man. I can't be running all over
the country to view the brainstorm of every
crackpot. I looked at his sample and I told my staff
to investigate it. That's all I could do. Even you
might understand that."

Simon stared at him thoughtfully through a couple of clouds of smoke. He was beginning to get an
odd feeling about this interview which fitted with
nothing that he had expected. Frank Imberline was
as pompous and phony as a bullfrog with a mega-
phone; his thinking appeared to be done in reso-
nant cliches, and he uttered them all the time as if
he were addressing a large rally in a public square.
And yet from the beginning his reaction to Simon's
presence had been one of righteous indignation and
not fear. It was true that the Saint hadn't waved a
knife under his nose or made any threatening
noises. But the Saint had also calmly admitted a
technical act of burglary, which there was no deny-

ing anyhow; and any normal citizen would have regarded such an intruder as at least a potentially dangerous screwball. Well, possibly Imberline was one of those men who are too obtuse to be subject to ordinary fear. But in that case, why hadn't he simply rung or called for help and had the Saint arrested?

Because he was more profoundly afraid that the Saint had something else up his sleeve? Or for some other reason?

Imberline was returning his scrutiny just as shrewdly. He took the cigar out of his mouth and bit off the end. "You tell me that Miss—er—Gray is a very attractive young woman," he said.

"She is."

"Young man, I'm going to ask *you* a question."

"Shoot."

"Is there any romantic reason for this interest of yours?"

The Saint shook his head.

"None at all."

"Have you invested any money in this so-called invention?"

"No."

Imberline struck a match and put it to the cigar.

"Well, then," he said in a gust of smoke, "what the hell are you here for?"

"That's a fair question," said the Saint. "I have some quaint reasons of my own for believing that this invention may have more in it than you think. If that's true, I'm as interested as any citizen in wanting to see something done about it. If there's any fake about it, I'm still interested—from another angle. And from that angle, I'd be even more interested if the invention was really good and there was a powerful and well-organized campaign of skullduggery going on to prevent anything being done about it."

"Why?"

"I've told you my name. But perhaps you'd know me better if I said—the Saint."

Imberline's cigar jerked in his mouth as his teeth clamped on it, and his eyes squeezed up again. But there was no change of color in the florid face. No —Frank Imberline, with or without a guilty conscience, wasn't panicked by shadows. He stared back at the Saint, without blinking, puffing smoke out of the side of his mouth in intermittent clouds.

"You're a crook," he said.

"If you'd care to put that in writing," said the Saint calmly, "I shall be very glad to sue you for libel. There isn't a single legal charge that can be brought against me—other than this little matter of breaking and entering tonight."

The other made a short impatient gesture.

"Oh, I'm sure you've been clever. And I've read some of that stuff about your Robin Hood motives. But your methods, sir, are not those which have been set up by our democratic constitution. The end does not justify the means. No individual has the right to take the law into his own hands. The maintenance of our institutions and our way of life, sir, rests upon the subordination of private prejudice to the authorised process of our courts."

He gave the pronouncement a fine oratorical rotundity, paused as if to allow the acclamation of an unseen audience to subside, and said abruptly: "However. Your suggestion that my Department could be influenced by anything but the best interests of the country is insulting and intolerable. I'm going to prove to you that you're talking a lot of crap."

"Good."

"You bring this Miss Gray to see me, and I'll prove to you that she has a chance to present her case if she's got one."

Simon could hardly believe his ears.

"Do you mean that?"

"What the hell are you talking about, do I mean it? Of course I mean it! I'm not condoning your behavior, but I do know how to put a stop to the sort of rumor you're starting."

"When? Tomorrow?"

"No. I'm leaving first thing in the morning for New York and Akron on Government business. But as soon as I get back. In a couple of days. Keep in touch with my office."

The Saint went on looking at him with a sense of deepening bafflement that had the question marks pounding through his head like triphammers. His blue eyes were cool and inscrutable, but behind the mask of his face that strange perplexity went on. If this was a stall to get him out of there and keep him quiet for a couple of days, perhaps while further shenanigans were concocted, it was still a perfect stall. There was still no way of exposing it except by waiting. Imberline had taken the wind out of his sails. But if it wasn't a stall . . . Simon found his head aching with the new incongruities that he would have to untangle if it wasn't a stall.

"Now get the hell out of here," Imberline said defiantly.

There was nothing else to do.

Simon stood up, crushed his cigarette in an ashtray, and hoped that his nonchalant impassivity had enough suggestion of postponed menace and loaded sleeves to conceal the completely impotent confusion of his mind. For perhaps the first time in his life he felt that he hadn't a single answer in him.

"Thank you," he said, and left the room like that.

He let himself out of the front door, and crossed the lawn diagonally towards the street, moving through the dark patches cast by the thick spruce trees with the silence that was as natural to him as breathing.

He was just emerging from the deepest gloom when he stumbled over somebody who had been taken unaware by his cat-like approach. The man he had bumped into straightened, squeaked, and vanished like a startled rabbit. But although he disappeared in the time it might take eyelash to meet eyelash in a slow blink, the Saint knew who he was. It was the funny little man, Sylvester Angert.

2

Simon Templar walked back to the Shoreham, conscious always of the movement of shadows about him. He knew he was wide open for a pot shot, but he had the idea that nobody wanted to kill him—yet. They might kill Madeline Gray, and her father, but not before they got the formula from one of the two. He himself was a recent nuisance, not yet thoroughly estimated; and the forces that were working against the Grays would hardly want to complicate their problem with a police investigation until they were convinced that there was no alternative.

He was a trifle optimistic in this prognosis, as it was soon to be demonstrated.

Madeline Gray opened her door when he gave the password he had written down, and he almost laughed at the solemn roundness of her eyes.

"I'm not a returning ghost," he said. "Come back

downstairs and I'll buy you another drink."

They walked down to his floor, and he waited until she was curled up on the sofa with her feet tucked under her and a Peter Dawson in her hand.

Then he said, without preface: "I've just been to see Imberline."

Her mouth opened and stayed open in an unfinished gasp of amazement and incredulity, and he had time to light a cigarette before she got it working again.

"H-h-how?"

"I burgled his house and walked in on him. Rather illegal, I suppose, but it suddenly seemed like such an easy way to cut out a lot of red tape and heel-cooling." The Saint grinned a little now in reminiscent enjoyment of his own simplifying impudence; and then without a change of that expression he added bluntly: "He says your father is a crackpot phony."

His eyes fastened on hers, and he saw resentment and anger harden the bewilderment out of her face.

"I told you Mr. Imberline has never seen a demonstration of Father's process. He doesn't dare, because of what our invention might do to the natural rubber business after the war."

"He says he told his staff to investigate it."

"His staff!" she snorted. "His stooges! Or maybe just some other men with their own axes to grind. Father met them, and wouldn't talk to them after they demanded to see the formula before they'd see a demonstration. I told you he isn't the most tactful person in the world. He suspected Imberline's men from the first, and he made no bones about throwing them out of the laboratory when they came up to Stamford."

"On the other hand, Imberline promised to give

you a hearing himself if I brought you to see him."

She couldn't be stunned with the same incredulity again, but it was as if she had been jarred again behind the eyes.

"He told you that?"

"Yes. In a couple of days. As soon as he gets back from a trip that he has to rush off to tomorrow."

She breathed quickly a couple of times, so that he could hear it, in a sort of jerky and frantic way.

"Do you think he meant it?"

"He may have. He didn't have to say that. He could have screamed bloody murder, thundered about the police, or told me to go to hell. But he didn't even try."

She put her glass down on the low table in front of her and rubbed her hands shakily together as if they felt clammy. Her lips trembled, and the voice that came through them had a tremor in it to match.

"I—I don't know what to say. You've been so wonderful—you've done so much—made everything seem so easy. I feel so stupid. I—I don't know whether I ought to kiss you, or burst into tears, or what. I don't know how to believe it."

He nodded.

"That," he said flatly, "is my problem."

"What did you do to persuade him?"

"Very little. It was too easy."

"Well, why do you think he did it?"

"I wish I knew." The Saint scowled at his cigarette. "He may have been scared of the trouble I might stir up—but he didn't look scared of anything. He may have been afraid that I really had something on him. He may be a very clever and a very cunning guy, and he may have been just getting himself elbow room to hit back with a real brick in his glove. He may be on somebody's pay-roll, and he may have to go back to his boss for orders when he's in a jam. He may just have a sort of caliph complex, and get a shot in his ego from making what he thinks is a grand eccentric gesture —something to make an anecdote out of and show what a big-minded down-to-earth democrat he is. All of that's possible. And none of it seems enough, somehow. . . . So I muddle and brood around, and I still come back to one other thing."

"What's that?"

He said: "How much of this persecution of you and your father is real? How much of that is crackpot, how much is imagination—and how much is fake?"

The new disbelief in her eyes was sharp with hurt.

"After all this—are you still thinking that?"

He gazed at her detachedly, trying to persuade himself that he could make the same decision that he would have made if she had been fat and fifty with buck teeth and a wart on her nose.

Then he stopped looking at her. He was not so hot at being detached. He strolled over to the window and gazed out at the panorama of distant lights beyond the grounds and the Park. . . .

Ping!

The glass in front of him grew an instantaneous spider-web around a neat round hole, and the plunk of the bullet lodging itself in the wall plaster some-where above and behind him came at about the same moment.

He was probably already in motion when he heard it, for his impressions seemed to catch up with it quite a little while later. And by that time he was spun around with his back to the wall between the two windows, temporarily safe from any more careless exposure, and looking at Madeline Gray's white face with a quite incorrigible silent laughter in his eyes.

"By God," he said, "even the Washington mosquitoes have war fever. They must be training to be dive bombers."

She looked up at the opposite wall, near the ceiling, where his glance had also gone to search for the scar of the shot. After a second or two she found her voice somewhere.

"Somebody shot at you," she said, and sounded as if she knew it was the only possible foolish thing to say.

"That would be another theory," he admitted.

"But where from?"

"From the grounds, or the Park. They had the window spotted, of course. I'm afraid I'm getting careless in my old age."

He reached sideways cautiously for the edge of the shade, and pulled it all the way down. Then he did the same thing for the other window. After that he felt free to move again.

"Won't you catch them, or—or something?"

He laughed.

"I'm not Superman, darling. By the time I got downstairs they could be blocks away. I should have known better—I was warned once, at least." Then his face was sober again. "But I guess the ungodly are still answering for you. If all this is fooling, it's certainly an awful complicated game."

She met his eyes with a visible tumult of thoughts that couldn't form into words.

Then, in the silence, the telephone rang.

Simon crossed to it and picked it up.

"This is Miss Brown of the Associated Press," it

said. "I heard that you were in town, and I wondered if you'd be terribly angry if I asked you for a short interview."

It was a light and engaging and unusually arresting voice, but Simon Templar had met specialised voices before.

"I don't know what you could interview me about," he said. "I'm thirty-five years old, I think J. Edgar Hoover is wonderful, I believe that drinking is here to stay, I want everyone to buy War Bonds, and I am allergic to vitamins. Beyond that, I haven't anything to say to the world."

"I'd only take a few minutes, really, and you wouldn't have to answer any questions you didn't like."

"Suppose you call me tomorrow and I'll see what I'm doing." he suggested, giving himself a mental memorandum to see that his telephone was cut off.

"Why, are you in bed already?"

The Saint's brows climbed fractionally and drew down again.

"When I was a girl that would have been called a rather personal question," he said.

"I'm downstairs in the lobby now," she said. "Why couldn't we get it over tonight? I promise you can throw me out as soon as you've had enough."

And that was when the last of the Saint's hesitations winked out like a row of punctured bubbles, so that he wondered how he could ever have wasted time on them.

For girl reporters in real life do not come as far as the lobby of their victim's hotel before they ask for an interview. Nor do they press for ordinary interviews in the middle of the night. Nor do they use a sexy voice and a faintly suggestive turn of phrase to wheedle their way into the presence of a reluctant subject.

The sublime certainty of his intuition crescendoed around him with the symphonic grandeur of a happy orchestra. The decision had been taken out of his hands. He could resist temptation just so long, but there was a limit to how much he could be pushed. The note he had found in his pocket had been bad enough. The encounter with the aspiring kidnappers had been worse. The episodes of Mr. Angert and Mr. Imberline had been a bonus of aggravation. To be potted at in his own window by a sniper was almost gross provocation, even if he was broad-minded enough to admit that it was his own fault for providing the target. But this—this was positively and finally going too far.

"Okay," he said in a resigned tone. "Come on up."

He put the telephone back in its cradle as gently as a mother laying down her first-born, and turned back to the girl with a smile.

"Go to your room again, Madeline," he said; and for the first time that evening the full gay carelessness of a Saintly lilt was alive and laughing in his voice. "Get your things packed. We're going to Connecticut tonight."

Her eyes were bewildered.

"But I have to see Mr. Imberline."

"I'll get you back here as soon as we've arranged a genuine appointment. But that won't be tomorrow. Meanwhile, I can't be in two places at once. And maybe your father needs looking after too." He grinned. "Don't bother about those private detectives. I'm sold—if you'll still buy me."

She laughed a little through uncertain lips.

"Are you very expensive?"

"Not if you buy your Peter Dawson wholesale. Now run along. And the same password applies. I'll be after you as soon as I'm through with this."

He had her arm and he was taking her to the door.

"What was that telephone call?" she asked. "And how do you know you're going to be all right?"

"That's what I'm going to find out," he said. "I won't be any help to you hiding in a cellar. But I'm firmly convinced that I was not destined to die in Washington. Not this week, anyhow . . . I'll see you soon, darling."

She stood in the doorway for a moment, looking at him; and then, suddenly and very quickly, she kissed him.

Then she was gone.

Simon went into the bedroom, opened a suitcase, and took out an automatic already nested in a spring holster. He slipped his arms through the harness, shrugged it into comfort, and went back into the living room and put his coat on again. It seemed like a slightly melodramatic routine; but the only reason why Simon Templar had lived long enough to become a legend before he was also a name on a tombstone was that he had never been coy about taking slightly melodramatic precautions. And in the complex and sinful world where he had spent most of his life, there were no guarantees that when an alluring feminine voice invited itself in on the telephone there would be an alluring feminine person on the doorstep when the doorbell next rang.

He just had time to light another cigarette and freshen his drink before that potential crisis was with him.

He opened the door with his left hand and swung it wide, standing well aside as he did so. But it was only a girl who matched the telephone voice who came in.

He risked one arm to reach across the opening and draw the door shut behind her, and he quietly set the safety lock as he did so.

After that, without the slightest relaxing of his vigilance, and still with that steady pressure of ghostly bullets creeping over his flesh, he followed her into the living-room and surveyed her again in a little more detail. She was tall and built with the kind of curvacious ripeness in which there is hardly a margin of a pound between perfection and excess. So far she was still within the precarious safety of the narrow margin, so that her figure was a startling excitement to observe. Her face was classically beautiful in a flawless peach-skinned way. She had natural blonde hair and rather light blue eyes that gave her expression a kind of passionate vagueness.

"All right, darling," said the Saint. "I'm in a hurry too, so we'll make it easy. Who sent you and what am I supposed to fall for?"

3

Her face was blank and innocent.

"I dont quite understand. I was just told to get an interview—"

"Let's save a lot of time," said the Saint patiently. "I know that you aren't from the AP, and probably your name isn't Brown either—but that's a minor detail. You can put on any act you like and talk from here to breakfast, but you'll never get anywhere. So let's start from here."

She regarded him quite calmly.

"You have very direct methods, haven't you?"

"Don't you think they cut the hell out of the overhead?"

She glanced placidly around the room, and observed the potable supplies on the side table. He was aware that she didn't miss the half-empty glass the Madeline Gray had left, either.

"I suppose you wouldn't like to offer me a drink?"

Without answering, he poured a highball and handed it to her.

"And a cigarette?"

He gave her one and lighted it.

"Now," he remarked, "you've had plenty of time to work on your story, so it ought to be good."

She laughed.

"Since you're so clever—you ought to be able to tell me."

"Very likely I can." He lighted another cigarette for himself. "You are either an Axis agent, a private crook, or a mildly enterprising nitwit. You may have fancier names for it, but it comes to the same thing. Once upon a time I'd have laid odds on the third possibility, but just recently I've gotten a bit skeptical."

"You make it sound awfully interesting. So what am I here for—as an Axis agent or a private crook?"

"That's a little more difficult. But I can think of the possibilities. You either came here to eliminate me—with or without outside cooperation—or to get information of one kind or another. Of course, there are gentle angles on both of those bright ideas, as well as the rough and noisy ones. We could stay up all night playing permutation and combinations. I was just curious to know what your script was."

"And if I don't tell you?"

"We'll just have to play it out," he said tiredly. "Go on. Shoot. Give me the opening line."

She tilted her head back, showing teeth as regular as a necklace of pearls.

"I think you're beautiful," she said.

"Thank you."

"You talk just like I imagined you would."

"That must be a great relief."

"You sound wildly exciting."

"Good."

"But I'm afraid I'm going to be a great disappointment."

"Are you?"

"I'm afraid I'm only a mildly enterprising nitwit."

He went on looking at her dispassionately.

"I adore you," she said.

"I adore me too," he said. "Tell me about you."

She tasted her drink.

"My name's Andrea Quennel."

It went through him like a chemical reaction, a sudden congealing and enveloping stillness. In an almost unreal detachment he observed her left hand. It wore no rings. He crossed over to her, and calmly took the purse from her lap and opened it. He found a compact with her initials on it, and didn't search any further.

"Satisfied?" she asked.

"You must be Hobart Quennel's daughter," he said.

"That's right. We came in just as Mr. Devan was driving off after he'd dropped you. He told us about your little excitement this evening. He hadn't thought anything about your name, but being a romantic soul of course I had to wonder at once if it was you. So I inquired at the desk, and it was."

She looked very pleased with herself, and very comfortable.

"That still doesn't tell me why you had to see me this way," he said.

"I wanted to meet you. Because I've been crazy about you for years."

"Why did you try to pretend to be a reporter?" She shrugged.

"You said it yourself, didn't you? I'm a mildly enterprising nitwit. So I don't want everyone to know what a nitwit I am. I suppose I could have made Mr. Devan call you up on some excuse and met you that way, but I try to let him think I'm halfway sane, because after all he does work for my father. And if I'd call you up and said I was dying to meet you I was sure you'd just send the house detective after me. So I thought I was being rather clever." Her face became quite empty and listless. "I guess I wasn't. I'm sorry."

Her vague light eyes studied him for a moment longer; and then she stood up.

"Anyway, I did get to meet you, just the same, so I think it was worth it . . . I'll get out of your way now."

He watched her. The curious inward immobility that had seized him when she told him her name had dissolved completely, but imperceptibly, so that he hadn't even noticed the change. But his brain was fluid and alive again now, as if all the cells in it were working like coordinated individuals, like bees in a hive.

He said: "Sit down, Andrea, and finish your drink."

She sat down, with a surprised expression, as if someone had pushed her. The Saint smiled.

"After all, you were enterprising," he murmured,

"so I'll forgive you. Besides, it's just occurred to me that you might be able to do something for me one of these days."

Her eyes opened.

"Could I? I'd do anything . . . But you're just kidding me. Nothing so marvelous as that could ever happen!"

"Don't be too sure."

"Do you often do that?—I mean, get perfect strangers to help you do things?"

"Not often. But sometimes. And anyway, perhaps by that time we won't be such strangers."

"I hope not," she said softly; and then she blinked. "This isn't happening to me," she said.

He laughed.

"What do you do—work for Quenco too?"

"Oh, no. I'm much too stupid. I just do nothing. I'm a very useless person, really. What would you want me to do for you?"

"I'll tell you when the time comes."

"I hope it'll be something exciting."

"It might be."

She leaned forward a little, watching him eagerly.

"Tell me—why did you think I might be an Axis agent? Were you expecting one?"

"It wasn't impossible," he said carefully.

"Are you working on some Secret Service job? And those men you had the fight with tonight . . . No, wait." She frowned, thinking. Somehow, although she said she was stupid, she managed to look quite intelligent, thinking. "Mr. Devan only thought of a hold-up. But he knew this girl you rescued—Madeline Gray. You see, I've got a memory like a parrot. Her father has an invention. Synthetic rubber. So the Gestapo or whatever it is want to get hold of it. So they think if they can kidnap his daughter they can make him tell. But you're looking after her, so they don't get away with it. So you think they'll be sending somebody to get rid of you. How's that?"

He blew a meticulously rounded smoke-ring.

"It's not bad."

"Is it right?"

"I can't answer for all of it. Madeline Gray, yes. Father makes synthetic rubber, yes. Try to kidnap daughter, yes. But who and why—that's something to make up our minds about slowly."

"Is that why you asked if I was an Axis agent or a private crook?" she said shrewdly.

The shift of his lips and eyebrows was cheerfully noncommittal.

"Wonderful weather we've been having," he said.

"But you were looking after her."

"I am looking after her," he said, without a trace of emphasis on the change of tense.

She pouted humorously.

"All right. I mustn't ask questions." She finished her drink, and gazed into the empty glass. "Couldn't we go somewhere and dance?" she said abruptly.

"No." He came up off the chairback that he had been propping himself on. "I'm sorry, but I've got to pack a couple of things. And then I'll be traveling."

She stood up.

"You mean you're leaving Washington?"

"Yes."

"Then how are we going to get to know each other better?"

"How does anyone find you?"

"You can call Daddy's office in New York. His secretary always knows where we are—he talks to her every day. I'll talk to her myself and ask her to tell you."

"Then it ought to be easy."

She hesitated.

"But where are you going?"

He thought it over before he answered.

"I'm going to see Calvin Gray, and I'm taking Madeline with me. I told you I was looking after them. I'd love to go dancing with you, Andrea, but this is business."

"Where does he live?"

"Near Stamford, Connecticut."

"We've got a place at Westport," she said lingeringly.

"Then we might run into each other some time," he smiled.

He took her to the door, and after she had gone he came back and poured himself another drink before he went to the telephone. He had to call three or four numbers before he located the man he wanted.

"Hullo, Ham," he said. "Simon. Sorry to interrupt you, but I'm going solo for a few days. I want a private plane to go to the nearest field to Stamford. Organize it for me, will you? I'll be at the airport in an hour."

"You don't want much, do you?"

"Only one of those little things that you handle so beautifully, comrade . . . Oh, and one other thing."

"I suppose you'd like Eleanor to come down and see you off."

"Get me some dossiers. Anything and everything you can dig up—including dirt. Airmail them to me at General Delivery, Stamford. Get the names. Calvin Gray, research chemist. A guy named Walter Devan, who works for Quenco." Simon lighted a cigarette. "Also Hobart Quennel himself, and his daughter Andrea."

He hung up, and sat for several moments, drawing steadily at his cigarette and watching the smoke drift away from his lips.

Then he went into the bedroom and started packing his bag, humming gently to himself as he moved about. He was traveling very light, and there wasn't much to do. He had practically finished when the telephone rang again, and he picked it up.

"Washington Ping-pong and Priority Club," he said.

"This is Madeline Gray," she said. "Are you still tied up?"

"No."

"Can you come up to see me, or shall I come down?"

He didn't need to be as sensitive as he was to feel the unnatural restraint in her voice.

"Is something going on," he asked quietly, "or can't you talk now? Just say Yes or No."

"Oh, yes, I can talk. There's nobody here. I suppose I'm just silly. But . . ." The pause was quite long. Then she went on, and her voice was still cold and level and sensible. "I've been trying to phone my father and let him know we're coming. But they say there's no answer."

Simon relaxed on the bed and flipped cigarette ash on the carpet.

"Maybe he's gone to a movie, or he's out with the boys analysing alcohol in one of the local saloons."

"He never goes out in the evening. He hates it.

Besides, he knew I was going to phone tonight. I was going to talk to him as soon as I'd seen Imberline. Nothing on earth would have dragged him out until he knew about that. Or do you think you've scared me too much?"

The Saint lay back and stared at the ceiling, feeling cold needles tiptoeing up his spine and gathering in spectral conclave on the nape of his neck.

4

Simon Templar checked his watch mechanically as the Beechcraft sat down on the runway at Armonk airport. One hour and fifteen minutes from Washington was good traveling, even with a useful tail wind, and he hoped that his haste hadn't ground too much life out of the machinery.

The pilot who was to take the ship back, who hadn't asked a single question all the way because he had been taught not to, said: "Good luck." Simon grinned and shook hands, and led Madeline Gray to the taxi that he had phoned to meet them.

As they turned east towards Stamford he was still considering the timetable. They could be at Calvin Gray's house in twenty minutes. Making about an hour and thirty-five minutes altogether. Only a few minutes longer than one of the regular airlines would have taken to make New York, even if there had been a plane leaving at the same time. Furthermore, he had left no loophole for the Ungodly to sabotage the trip, or to interfere with him in any way before he got to his destination. They couldn't have intercepted him at any point, because they couldn't have discovered his route before it was too late.

As for any other connections that the Ungodly

could have used, it would have taken an hour to drive from New York to Stamford, or fifty minutes on a fast train—ignoring such delays as phone calls to start the movement, or the business of getting a vehicle to drive in, or the traveling to and from railroad stations and the inconsiderate tendency of railroads not to have trains waiting on a siding at all hours ready to pull out like taxis off a rank.

He had tried to explain some of this to the girl while they were flying.

"If anything *has* happened to Daddy," she said now, "there were people there already."

"Then whatever happened has happened already," he said, "and nobody on earth could have caught up with it. I thought of phoning somebody to go out from New York, but they mightn't have gotten here any sooner than we have. I could have phoned the Stamford Town Police, but what could we have told them? So the telephone doesn't answer. They'd have said the same as I said. By the time we'd gotten through all the arguing and rigmarole, it could have been almost as late as this by the time they got started. If they ever got started."

"Maybe I'm just imagining too much," she said.

He didn't know. He could just as easily have been imagining too much himself. He had spent a lot of time trying to get his own mind straight.

He said, because it helped to crystallise his ideas to talk aloud: "The trouble is that we don't even know who the Ungodly are, or what they're working towards . . . Suppose they were private crooks. An invention like this could be worth a fortune. They'd want to get the formula—just for dough. All right. They might kidnap you, so that they could threaten your father with all kinds of frightful things that might happen to you if he didn't give them the secret. They might kidnap him, and try to torture it out out of him.''

He felt her flesh tighten beside him.

''But there have also been these accidents you told me about. Wrecking his laboratory. Sabotage. It's a nice exciting word. But where would it get them—in the end?''

She said: ''If they were spies—''

''If they were spies,'' he said, ''they wouldn't be blowing up a laboratory. They might break into it to see what they could see. But they wouldn't destroy it, because they want the work to go on. They just want the results. And if they wanted to kidnap you or your father to squeeze a formula out of you with horsewhips and hot irons—they'd have tried it long before this. You wouldn't have been hard to snatch.''

''Well,'' she said, ''they could just be saboteurs. They warned me not to try and see Mr. Imberline. They might just want to stop us getting anywhere.''

''Then both of you would have been crated and under grass by this time,'' he said coldbloodedly. ''Killing is a lot easier than kidnapping, and when you get into the class of political and philosophical killers you are talking about a bunch of babies who never went to Sunday School. That's the whole thing that stops me. What goes with this pulling of punches—this bush league milquetoast skullduggery?''

He went on nagging his mind with that proposition while the taxi turned up the Merritt Parkway and presently branched off again to the right up a meandering lane that brought them to a stone gateway and through that up a short trim drive to the front of a comfortably spacious New England frame house. He had a glimpse of white shingled walls and green shingled roofs and gables as the taxi's headlights swept over them, and he saw that there were lights behind some of the curtains. For a moment her hand was on his arm, and he put his own hand over it, but neither of them said anything.

She opened the front door while he was paying off the driver, and he carried their bags up the path of light to the hall and joined her there.

She called: "Daddy!"

They could hear the taxi's wheels crunching out off the gravel, and the hum of its engine fading down the lane, leaving them alone together in the stillness.

"Daddy," she called.

She went through an open door into the living-room, and he put the bags down and followed her. The room was empty, with one standard lamp burning beside the piano.

She went out again quickly.

He stayed there, lighting a cigarette and taking in the scene. It was a livable kind of room, with built-in bookshelves and plenty of ashtrays and not too fancy chintz covers on the chairs, a pleasant compromise between interior decorating and masculine comfort. There were no signs of violence or disorder, but there were rumples in various cushions where they had been sat on since the room was last done over. There was a pipe in one of the ashtrays by the fireplace: he went over and felt the bowl, and it was quite cold. He wondered how long a pipe bowl would stay warm after it was put down.

A telephone stood on the same table. He picked it up, and heard the familiar tone of a clear line. Just to make sure, he dialed a number at random, and heard the ringing at the other end, and then the click of the connection, and a gruffly sleepy male voice that said "Yes?"

"This is Joe," said the Saint momentously. "You'd better start thinking fast. Your wife has discovered everything."

He hung up, and turned to Madeline Gray as she came back into the room.

"The phone is working," he said casually. "There's nothing wrong with the line."

"Come with me," she said.

He took her arm and crossed the hall with her. They looked into the dining room, sedate and barren like any dining room between meals. They went on into the kitchen. It was clean and spotless, inhabited only by a ticking clock on a shelf.

"He's been here," she said.

"Would he have had dinner?"

"I couldn't tell."

"What about servants?"

"We haven't had anyone living in for a couple of weeks, and we weren't going to do anything about it until I got back from Washington. Daddy couldn't have been bothered with interviewing them and breaking them in. I got him a girl who used to work for us, who got married and lives quite close by. She could have got him his dinner and cleaned up and gone home."

After that there was a study lined with ponderous and well-worn books, and featuring a couple of filing cabinets and a big desk littered with papers as the principal movable furniture. It was fairly messy, in a healthy haphazard way.

Simon went to one of the filing cabinets, and pulled open a drawer at random. The folders looked regular enough, to anyone who hadn't lived with the system.

He turned from there to glance over the desk. He only saw a disarray of letters, circulars, cryptic memoranda, abstruse pamphlets, and assorted manuscript.

"How does it look to you?" he asked.

"About the same as usual."

"You must have lived with some of this stuff. Does any of it look wrong?"

She skimmed through the filing drawer that he had opened, and turned over some of the papers on the desk. After that she still looked blank and helpless.

"I couldn't possibly say. He's so hopelessly untidy when he isn't being fanatically neat."

Simon stared at the desk. He didn't know Calvin Gray's habits, or anything about his work and interests. He knew that it was perfectly possible to search files and papers without leaving a room looking as if a cyclone had gone through it.

Anyway, what would anyone have been searching for? Nobody would have been expected to keep a precious secret formula in an open filing cabinet, or sandwiched between tax demands and seed catalogs on top of a desk . . . And still he had that exasperating feeling of underlying discord, of some factor that didn't explain itself or didn't connect, as if he was trying to force everything into one or two wrong theories, when there was still a right theory that would have accommodated everything, only he had been too blind to see it yet.

"Let's see everything," he said shortly.

They went upstairs and saw bedrooms. Madeline Gray's room. Calvin Gray's room. A couple of guest rooms. Bathrooms. Everything looked ordinary and orderly. It was a nice well-kept house.

"So he isn't here," said the Saint. "There's no blood and no smashed windows and no dead bodies in any of the closets. He went out and left the lights on. Why shouldn't he go out and leave the lights on?"

He didn't know whether he was trying to console her or whether he was arguing with himself. He knew damn well that it was perfectly simple to kidnap a man without wrecking his house. You just walked in on him and stuck a gun in his ribs and said "Come for a walk, pal," and nine times out of ten that was all the commotion there was going to be.

"There's still the laboratory," she said in a small voice; and he caught at that for the moment's reprieve.

"Why didn't you show me that before?"

She took him out of the house, and they walked by a winding path through tall slender trees whose delicate upper branches lost themselves in the darkness beyond the glow of his pencil flashlight.

The laboratory had been invisible from the house and the driveway, and they came on it suddenly in a shadowy clearing—a long white modernistic building with a faint glow from inside outlining the venetian windows. She led him to the door, and they went into a tiny hall. A door that stood ajar on one side disclosed tiled walls and a washbasin and shower.

Beyond the little hall, the laboratory was a long sanitary barn with a single lamp burning overhead and striking bright gleams from glass tubes and retorts and long shelves of neatly labeled bottles and porcelain-topped benches and stranger pieces of less describable apparatus. But nothing was broken, and everything seemed reasonably in order. Only there was no one there.

"Does this look all right too?" he asked.

"Yes."

He surveyed the details as meaninglessly as any other layman would have surveyed a chemical laboratory. If you were going to produce any brilliant observation in a setting like that, you had to be a master chemist too. And he wasn't. He wondered if any detective really ever knew everything, so that he could immediately start finding incongruities in any kind of technical setup, like super sleuths always could in stories.

"You could make rubber here?" he said.

"Of course."

There must have been more doubt in his face than he meant to have there, or else he just looked blank because he was thinking along other lines, or else she also wanted to keep her mind busy along other lines.

"I could show you now," she said.

It didn't seem important, but it was another escape.

"Show me," he said.

She went and fetched bottles from the shelves. Some of them were unlabeled. She measured things in beakers and test tubes. She carried mixtures to a table where an elaborate train of processing gear was already set up. She poured a quantity of sawdust from an old coffee can into a glass bowl, lighted a burner under it, and began to blend it with various fluids. She looked as prosaic and efficient and at home as a seasoned cook mixing pancakes.

The Saint hitched one hip on to another bench and watched. It was no use his trying to look wise and intelligent about it. He had more than the average background of ordinary chemistry, as he had of a hundred other unlikely subjects, but things went on in this production line that were utterly out of his depth. He saw fluids moving through tubes, and coils and bubbling in flasks, changing color and condensing and precipitating, and finally flowing into a small peculiar encased engine that looked as if it might house some kind of turbine, from which came a low smooth hum and a sense of dull heat. At the other end of this engine projected a long narrow troughed belt running over an external pulley; and over this belt began to creep a ribbon of the same shiny pale translucent orange-tinted stuff that she had shown him in the dining room of the Shoreham. She tore off the strip when there was about a couple of feet of it, and gave it to him; and he felt it between his fingers and stretched it as he had done before. It was still warm, and smelled a little like wet leather and scorched wool.

"It seems like a wonderful thing," he said. "But it looks a little more complicated than the bathtub proposition you were talking about."

She was methodically stopping the machinery and turning off burners.

"Not really," she said. "In terms of a big industrial plant, it's almost so simple that a village plumber could put it together."

"But even a simple plant on a large scale costs a lot of money. Does your father want the WPB to go into production on their own, or is he rich enough to start off by himself?"

"We aren't quite as rich as that. But if the Government went into it they'd give us a loan, and it wouldn't be any problem to raise the private capital. In fact, we'd probably have to hire guards to

keep the investors away." She smiled at him wanly.
"It's too bad I didn't meet you before, isn't it? You
could have come in on the ground floor and made a
fortune."

"I can just see myself at any board meeting," he
said.

Then they were really looking at each other
again, and the fear was back in her eyes and he was
afraid to laugh at it any more.

"What do you think has happened?" she asked;
and he straightened up and trod on the butt of his
cigarette.

"Let's go back to the house," he said roughly.

They went out, putting out the lights and closing
the door after them.

As they went through the tall arched tunnel of
leaves again her hand slid into the crook of his
elbow, and he pressed it a little against his side from
sympathy, but he was still thinking coldly and from
quite a distance. He said: "Did you lock the door?"

"I don't have the key."

"When we got to the house, how did you let
yourself in?"

"I just went in. The door wasn't locked."

"Isn't it ever locked?"

"Hardly ever. Daddy can't be bothered with keys
—he's always losing them. Besides why should we
lock up? We haven't anything worth stealing, and
who'd be prowling around here?"

"You said things had happened to the laboratory
before."

"Yes, but it's got so many windows that anybody
could break in if they really wanted to."

"So anybody could have walked in on your father
at any time tonight."

"Yes."

There wasn't any more to say. They went back
into the house, and into the comfortable living-
room with the cold pipe in the ashtray, and passed
the time. He strummed the piano, and parodied a
song or two very quietly, and she sat in one chair
after another and watched him. And all the time he
knew that there wasn't anything to do. Or to say, at
that moment.

It got to be later.

He took their bags upstairs, and put hers in her
room and chose himself a guest room opposite, with
a door directly facing hers across the corridor. He
opened his own bag before he came down again
and fixed drinks for both of them. Into her drink he
put a couple of drops from a phial that he brought
down with him.

Very quickly the hot bright strain went out of her
eyes, and she began yawning. In a little while she
was fast asleep. He carried her upstairs and put her
in her bed, and then he went across to his own room
and took off most of his clothes and lay down on the
bed with his automatic tucked under the edge of
the mattress close to his right hand, and switched
off the lights. He didn't think it was at all likely that
the Ungodly could get around to organising another
routine so soon, but he always preferred to overrate
the opposition rather than underrate them. He was
awake for a long time; and when he finally let himself sink into a light doze the first pallor of dawn
was creeping into the room, and he knew that he
had been wrong about the bush-league skullduggery and that Calvin Gray was not coming home
unless somebody fetched him.

3

How Madeline Gray was Persuaded to Eat, and Mr. Angert gave it Up.

It was half-past eight when Simon Templar woke up. He lay in bed for a few minutes, watching fleecy white clouds drift across the blue sky outside the windows, and reviving the thoughts on which he had fallen asleep. They didn't look any different now.

He got up and put on a robe and went out into the corridor. It was nothing but a kind of last-ditch wishfulness that made him go quietly into Calvin Gray's bedroom. But the bed hadn't been slept in, and the room was exactly as he had last seen it. He knew all the time that it would be like that, of course. If Calvin Gray had come home with the milkman, the Saint was sure that he would have heard him—he had been alert all night, even in his sleep, for much stealthier sounds than that would have been. But at least, he reflected wryly, he had forestalled a self-made charge of jumping to conclusions.

He went back to his own room, shaved, showered, and dressed, and went downstairs.

The table was laid with one place for breakfast in the dining room, and there were sounds of movement in the kitchen.

Simon pushed through the swing door, and stopped. A rosy-cheeked young woman with dark curly hair and an apron looked up at him with slightly startled eyes as he came in. She was small and nicely plump, in a way that would obviously become stout and matronly exactly when you would expect.

"Hullo," he said pleasantly. "Don't be scared. My name's Templar, and I came up from Washington with Miss Gray last night."

"Oh," she said. "I'm Mrs. Cook. I just work here. You did scare me for a minute, though."

He realised that since they had failed to talk to Calvin Gray there was no reason for anyone to expect them there. In fact, no one knew of their movement except Hamilton and the taxi driver who had brought them in from the airport. The driver might or might not talk or think anything of it. But at least it would take the Ungodly a little while to pick up the scent, which would be no disadvantage.

"I'm sorry," he said. "What are the chances for breakfast?"

"I'll set some more places."

"Miss Gray was pretty tired out last night. I'm hoping she'll sleep late."

"The Professor's usually up before this," she said. "He must have been working late."

The Saint had a friendly and engaging ease, whenever he wanted to use it, which made it seem the most natural thing in the world for anyone to keep on talking to him. He used that effortless receptiveness now, as a happy substitute for more tiresome and elaborate methods.

He said quite conversationally: "The Professor wasn't in last night."

"Wasn't he? He's nearly always in."

"We tried to phone him from Washington to say we were on our way, but the number didn't answer."

"Was that very late? I was here until about nine o'clock."

"It was later than that."

"I gave him his dinner at seven-thirty, and then I had to wash up. He was in the living-room, reading, when I went home."

"He didn't say anything about going out?"

"No. But I didn't ask him."

"He didn't have any visitors?"

"Not while I was here."

"Maybe he's been going out a bit while Miss Gray's been away."

"Oh, no, sir. The Professor's never been one for going out—"

It was only then that she began to be dimly aware of what his innocent questions were leading to. A trace of puzzlement crept into her eyes.

"Anyway," she said, almost defiantly, "he's sure to be down soon."

The Saint shook his head.

"I'm afraid he isn't, Mrs. Cook," he said quietly. "He didn't come in at all last night. His bed hasn't been slept in. And he's not in the house now."

She stopped on her way into the dining room with a handful of knives and forks and spoons, and stared at him blankly.

"You mean he isn't here at all?"

"That's right."

"Wasn't he expecting you?"

"No. I told you, we tried to phone, but we couldn't get him."

"Didn't he leave a note or anything?"

"No."

Her eyes began to get very wide.

"You don't think anything's happened to him, do you?"

"I don't know," said the Saint frankly. "It does look a little peculiar, doesn't it? The man just walks out of the house without a word or a message to anyone, and doesn't come back. Some people do things like that all the time, but you say he wasn't that type.

"Is Miss Gray worried about him?—I expect she is."

"Wouldn't you be?"

She began mechanically setting other places at the table, more as if she was going through a routine of habitual movements than as if she was thinking about what she was doing. "I expect somebody called him and had him go into New York on business after I'd left, and he was kept late and had to stay over," she said, seeming to reassure herself as much as her audience. "He'll probably be home before lunch-time, and if he isn't he'll phone. He wouldn't stay away without letting me know he wouldn't be back for dinner."

"Do you know where he usually stayed in New York?"

"He always stopped at the Algonquin. But he might have stayed with whoever he was with."

In a little while this mythical character would be as satisfactory as a real person.

"Maybe," said the Saint adaptively. "I'll have some eggs and bacon as soon as they're ready."

He went out and found the telephone in the living room, and called New York. The Algonquin Hotel informed him that nobody of the name of Calvin Gray had registered there the night before.

He lighted a cigarette and strolled out of the house. Sunlight made crazy fretwork patterns through the leaves of the surrounding trees, and flowers in well-kept beds splashed daubs of gay color against the white of the house and the green of square-trimmed hedges. The landscape fulfilled all the promise of the flashlight glimpses he had had the night before. The air was still cool, and there were clean and slightly damp sweet smells in it. It was a very pleasant place—a place that had been created for and that still nursed its memories of a gracious way of living that the paranoia of an unsuccessful housepainter was trying to destroy.

It seemed a long way from there to the thunder and flame of slaughter and destruction that ringed the world. And yet while that war went on Simon Templar could only acknowledge the peace and beauty around him with his mind. He had no ease in his heart to give to the enjoyment of the things he loved like that. No man had, or could have, until the guns were silent and the droning wings soared on the errands of life instead of death . . .

And perhaps even the tranquil scene in which he stood was part of a battlefield that the history books would never mention, but where uncountable decisions in Europe and the Orient might be lost or won.

He walked slowly around the house, his hands in his pockets and his eyes ranging over the ground. He would have missed nothing that could have told him a story, but it was a fruitless trip. The gravel drive registered no tire prints; there were no footprints in flower beds, no conveniently dropped handkerchiefs or hats or wallets. Not even a button. The only consolation was that he wasn't disappointed. He hadn't hopefully expected anything. It would have been dangerously like a trite detective story if he had found anything. But he had made the effort.

And it left him with nothing but the comfortless certainty that he had no material clues of any kind at all.

He went back into the house, and entered the dining room just as Mrs. Cook was putting a plate of sturdy eggs and crisp aromatic bacon on the table.

"That looks wonderful," he said. "It might even put a spark of life into my dilapidated brain."

It was typical of him that he started on the meal with as much zest as if he had nothing more important than a day's golf on his mind. He knew that he would solve no problems by starving himself; but unlike most men, he found that elementary argument quite sufficient to let him eat with unalloyed enjoyment.

He was halfway through when Madeline Gray came in.

She wore a simple cotton dress that made her look very young and tempting, but her face was pale and her eyes were bright with strain.

"Hullo," he said, so naturally that there might have been nothing else to say. "How did you sleep?"

"Like a log." She stood looking at him awkwardly. "Did you put something in that nightcap?"

"Yes," he said directly. "You'd never have gone to sleep without it."

"I know. It certainly worked. But it's left me an awful head."

"Take an aspirin."

"I have."

"Then you'll feel fine in a few minutes. You should have turned over and gone to sleep again."

"I couldn't."

Mrs. Cook came in from the kitchen and said with excessive cheeriness: "Good morning, Miss Gray. And what would you like for breakfast?"

"I don't feel like anything, thanks."

"You eat something," said the Saint firmly. "There are going to be things to do, and even you can't keep going on air and good intentions. Bring her a nice light omelette, Mrs. Cook. Then I'll hold her mouth open and you can slide it in."

Madeline Gray sat down at the table, and her eyes clung to the Saint with a kind of hopeless tenacity, as if he were the only thing that could hold her mind up to the verge of normality.

"My father didn't come home," she said flatly.

"No," The Saint was deliberately as quiet and impersonal as a doctor reporting on a case. "And you might as well have the rest of it now and get it over with. I called the Algonquin, which is where Mrs. Cook said he always stayed, and he wasn't there last night either."

"He must have stayed with his friend," Mrs. Cook said. "Whoever he went to see. Any minute now he'll be calling up—" The telephone rang while she was saying it.

Madeline ran.

And in a few moments she was back again, with the light out of her eyes.

"It's for you," she said tonelessly. "From Washington."

Simon went into the living-room.

"Hamilton," said the phone. "I wondered if I'd find you there. About those dossiers you asked for. I happen to have a man flying to New York this afternoon. If you're in a hurry for them, you can meet him there and get them this evening."

"When will he be there?"

"He should get in before five."

"I'll meet him at five o'clock in the men's bar of the Roosevelt."

"All right. He'll find you."

"There are a couple of other things, while you're talking," said the Saint. "You can add a little bit to his luggage. I want one more dossier. On Frank Imberline."

"That's easy. I'm a magician. All I have to do is wave a wand."

"Imberline left for New York and points west this morning—or so he told me. You can check on that. And if he's stopping over in New York, find out where he can be located."

"There aren't any other little jobs you want done, by any chance?"

"Yes. Get me okayed right away with the nearest FBI office to Stamford. I'll find out where it is. I think I'm going to have to talk to them."

"You aren't telling me you've got more on your hands than you can hold?"

"I'm having so much fun being almost legal," said the Saint. "It's a new experience. You'll be hearing from me."

He hung up, and went back to face Madeline Gray's unspoken questions.

He shook his head.

"Just one of those things," he said.

He sat down again; and Mrs. Cook retired reluctantly into the kitchen.

Simon faced the girl across the table. He picked up his knife and fork and made a fresh start on his meal before he said any more.

"Let's get our chins up and take it," he said. "You have got something to worry about. But we're going to try and do things about it. So far, the Ungodly have had practically all the initiative. Now we've got to have some of our own."

"But who are the—the Ungodly? If we only knew—"

That was as much as he needed. He talked, ramblingly and glibly, while he finished his plate, and then through coffee and cigarettes while the girl picked at the omelette that Mrs. Cook brought in to her. He discussed all the dramatis personae again, and an assortment of speculations about them. He said absolutely nothing that was new or worth recording here; but it sounded good at the time. And gradually he saw a trace of color creep into her face, and a shade of expression stir in her occasional replies, as he forced her mind to move and coaxed her with infinite subtlety out of the supine listlessness that had threatened to lock her in a stupor of inert despair. She even ate most of the omelette.

So that an hour later she was smoking a cigarette and listening to him quite actively, while he was saying: "There's one thing you'll notice about this. Every single person we've mentioned has been a good solid citizen with lots of background—except perhaps the quaint little Angert body. There hasn't been one grunt of a guttural accent, or one hint of the good old Gestapo clumping around in its great big boots. And yet if all these things have been going on, that'd be the first automatic thing to look for. Now if the Awful Aryans have got any—"

He stopped talking at the change in her face. But she was not looking at him. Her eyes were directed past his shoulder, towards the window behind him.

"Simon," she said, "I saw somebody moving out there among the trees, towards the laboratory. And it looked like someone I know."

2

The Saint turned and looked, but he could see nothing now—only a fragment of a roof and a glimpse of white walls between layers of leafy branches.

"A friend of yours?" he said sharply.

"No. It looked like—Karl."

"And who's Karl?"

"He was Daddy's assistant for a while, until we let him go."

"Where did he come from?"

"He was a refugee from somewhere—Czechoslovakia, I think. But he speaks perfect English. He was raised here, and then he went home after he was grown up, but he didn't like it so much so he came back."

"How long ago was this?"

"Oh, about a month ago. I mean when he left . . . But it's funny, I was thinking about him last night."

The Saint was still watching through the window, but he had seen no movement.

"Why?" he asked.

"Well, it seems silly, but . . . One of those men who tried to kidnap me last night—the tall one— there was something about his eyes, and the way he carried himself. It reminded me of someone. I couldn't think who it was, and it was bothering me. When I woke up this morning it came to me in a flash. He reminded me of Karl.''

"That," said the Saint, "is really interesting."

He turned and glanced at her again. She was still looking past him, half frowning, perplexed and uncertain of herself.

"What was the rest of his name?" he asked.

"Morgen."

Simon put out his cigarette.

"I think," he said, "it might be fun to talk to Comrade Morgen."

She stood up when he did and started to go with him, but he checked her with a hand on her arm.

"No, darling," he said. "For one thing, I'd rather surprise him. For another thing, if it really is Karl, and not just Karl on your mind, there may be a little horseplay when we meet. And lastly, I'd rather keep you out of sight as much as possible—for all purposes. In fact, I don't even want you to answer the telephone again. And if anyone does call except your father, tell Mrs. Cook to say you're still in Washington." He smiled at her confusion. "You forget that at this moment, the Ungodly don't know where you are. And the longer that lasts, the longer it'll be before I have to worry about your health again."

He went out of the house, crossed the driveway, and moved off among the trees.

The laboratory was on the other side of the house and in the opposite direction from the way he set off; and he made a wide circle to approach it from the far side—the side from which no intruder would be expecting an interruption.

His feet made no sound on the grass, and he

slipped through shrubbery and woodland with the phantom stealth of an Indian scout. He had an instinct for cover and terrain that was faultless and effortless; not once after he merged into the landscape was he exposed from any angle from which he could anticipate being watched for.

And under the cool efficiency of his movements he could feel a faint tingle along his veins that was his prescience of the disintegration of inaction and the promise of pursuit and fight. If Madeline Gray hadn't imagined what she saw, and there actually was an uninvited visitor out there, he would certainly be an interesting character to hold converse with —wherever he came from. And if the visitor really was a man with the dubious name and history of Karl Morgen, he might be the one missing quantity that Simon had just been idly complaining about. If, wildly and gorgeously beyond that, he crowned everything by proving to be one of the frustrated kidnappers of the night before—then indeed there would be moments of great joy in store. Anything so perfect as that seemed almost too much to expect; and yet, if even a fraction of those exquisite possibilities came true, it would still be more than enough to justify the tentative rapture that was stealing along the Saint's relaxed and tranquil nerves. He had always hated fighting in the dark, waiting to be shot at, the whole negative and passive rigamarole of puzzling and guessing and weighing of abstractions: if there was an end of that now, even for a little while, it would be a beautiful interlude . . .

Towards the end of his excursion, a tall cypress hedge offered perfect invisibility. He went along the edge of a field of oat hay for a hundred yards, and squeezed through another gap in the hedge into the concealment of a clump of rhododendron bushes. The laboratory building was so close then that he could see the roof over the top of his shelter.

Working around to the limit of his cover, he was finally able to sight one of the windows through the thinning fringe of leaves.

He saw more than the window. He saw through it. And all the inside of him became blissfully quiet as he saw that at least a part of his prayers had been granted.

There was a man in the laboratory.

And more than that, it wasn't just any man.

Simon couldn't see any details clearly in the darker interior, but he was able to distinguish a rough triangle of solid color where the lower part of the man's face should have been. Perhaps that crude disguise even helped the identification, by repeating a remembered pattern. The man's silhouette was clear enough. He looked tall, and the outlines and carriage of his broad square shoulders were freshly etched on the Saint's memory.

It was one of the ambitious abductors of Washington.

"So after all," said the Saint reverently, to his immortal soul, "sanctity does have its rewards."

The man seemed to be searching, methodically and without haste, as if he felt reasonably confident that he was not likely to be disturbed.

Simon drew back, and circled the other way around the rhododendrons, towards the corner of the building. The cover grew very low towards the corner, but by going flat on his stomach he was able to come up against the next wall, which had no windows in it. A few strides took him to a second corner; then he had to travel on his toes and fingertips again, stretched low like a lizard, to pass well below the front windows. Then he was at the door.

As he was rising, he paused when his eye reached the level of the keyhole. He could see through the tiny hall, and framed directly beyond it the man stood at one of the work-benches, facing towards him and studying something in a test tube.

Simon waited.

Presently the man put down the test tube and moved away, passing out of sight into another part of the laboratory.

The Saint straightened up.

He took the gun out of his shoulder holster and thumbed off the safety catch with his right hand while his left turned the door handle and eased the door open. The hinges revolved without a creak. He crossed the hallway in three soundless steps, and stood just inside the laboratory.

"Hullo, Karl," he said softly.

3

The man whirled at his voice, and then stood rigidly as the Saint moved his automatic very slightly to draw attention to its place in the conference.

"Looking for something?" Simon inquired politely.

The man didn't answer. Above the fold of the handkerchief that crossed his nose, his eyes were cold and ugly. The Saint had no more doubt whatever about one part of his identification. He wouldn't forget those eyes. They were the kind that didn't like anybody, and wanted to show it. They were the kind of eyes that the Saint loved to be disliked by.

"Suppose you take the awning off your kisser," Simon suggested, "and let's really get acquainted.

The man finally spoke.

"Suppose I don't."

If there had been any doubt left, it would have ended then. That hoarse cavernous voice was recorded in the Saint's memory as accurately as the eyes.

"If you don't," Simon said definitely, "I'll just have to shoot it off. Like this."

The gun in his hand coughed once, a crisp bark of power that slammed the eardrums, and the bullet ruffled the cloth over one of the man's ears before it spanged into the wall behind him. The man ducked after the bullet had gone by, and felt the side of his head with an incredulous hand. His forehead was three shades paler.

"Please," said the Saint.

He was not particularly concerned about noise any more. The windows were closed, and they were far enough from the house to be alone even for shooting purposes.

The man put his hands up slowly and untied the handkerchief behind the back of his head, revealing the rest of his face. He had a short beak of a nose and a square bony chin, and the mouth between them was thin and bracketed with deep vertical wrinkles. And the Saint knew him that way, too.

He had been a silent member of Frank Imberline's entourage at the Shoreham the night before.

He certainly got around.

One of his hands was moving self-consciously towards his pocket with the crumpled handkerchief, and the Saint said gently: "No, brother. Just hold it. Because if you tried a fast draw I might have to kill you, and then we wouldn't be able to talk without a medium; and I'm fresh out of mediums."

The movement stopped; and Simon smiled again.

"That's better. Now will you turn around?" The man obeyed. "Now walk backwards towards me."

The man shuffled back, dragging his feet reluctantly. When he was still six feet away, the Saint took two noiseless strides to meet him. Without changing his grip on his gun, he brought up his right hand and smashed the butt down on the back of the man's head. The man's knees buckled, and he fell forward on to his hands. Simon trod hard on the small of his back and flattened him. Then he came down on him with his knees.

He dropped his gun into a side pocket, grasped the lapels of the man's coat, and hauled it back over the man's shoulders to the level of his elbows. In a few lightning movements he emptied the man's pockets. He got a short-barreled revolver from one hip, and a blackjack from the other. The other pocket yielded very little—a ten-dollar bill, some small change, a car key, one of those pocket-knives that open up into the equivalent of a small chest of tools, and a thin wallet.

Simon gathered up the revolver, the blackjack, the knife, and the wallet, and retreated with them to the nearest work-bench. He put the revolver and the knife in another of his pockets. Then he took out his own automatic again and kept it in his hand. He sat side-saddle on the bench while he emptied the wallet. It contained three new twenty-dollar bills, a couple of stamps, the stub of a Pullman ticket, a draft card with a 4-F classification, and a New York driving license.

Both the draft card and driving license bore the name of Karl Morgen.

"Karl," said the Saint softly, "it was certainly

nice of you to drop in."

The man on the floor groaned and struggled to get his head off the ground.

Simon Templar fished out a cigarette and then a book of matches. He thumbed one of the matches over until he could rub the head on the striking pad one-handed. His eyes and his gun stayed watchfully on his prisoner. And all of him was awake with a great and splendiferous serenity.

If there could have been anything better than a hundred per cent fulfillment of the wildest possibilities he had dreamed of, he had been modest enough not to ask for it.

He could get along very beautifully with this much.

Karl Morgen. A man who had something to do with Imberline. A man who could be used for kidnaping. A man who had once worked for Calvin Gray. A man of very questionable antecedents. A man who might tie many curious things together. All combined in one blessed bountiful bonanza.

The Saint exhaled smoke and regarded him almost affectionately.

He said: "Get up."

Morgen had his head off the ground. He got his elbows under him and hunched his back. Then he gathered in his long legs. Somehow he got himself together and crawled up off the floor. He stood unsteadily, clutching the end of the work-bench, for support.

"Karl," said the Saint, "you used to work here."

"So what?"

"Why did you come back?"

The man's eyes were unflinchingly malevolent.

"That's none of your business, bud."

"Oh, but it is. Where were you last night?"

Morgen took his time.

Then he said: "In Washington."

"So you were. You were in the dining room of the Shoreham with Frank Imberline."

"That's no crime."

"We got a bit crowded, and you slipped a note in my pocket."

"I did not."

"The note said 'Mind your own business.' "

"Why don't you do that, bud?"

The Saint was still patient.

"Where were you after that?"

Again that deliberate pause. This wasn't a man who panicked. He thought all around what he was going to say before he said it.

"I was with a friend. Playin' cards."

"You were with a friend. But you weren't playing cards. You were trying to kidnap Miss Gray. That was when we met again."

"You'll have to prove that, bud."

"Both Miss Gray and I are ready to identify you."

"And my friend will say we were playin' cards."

"Quite a while after that," Simon continued unperturbed, "did you by any chance take a long shot at me through my window at the Shoreham?"

"No."

Simon inhaled thoughtfully.

"No, maybe that wasn't you. That was probably your chunky friend." He glanced down at the Pullman stub for a moment. "You came up on the sleeper last night, so you'd have been headed for the station by that time."

"It's a free country."

"I didn't think you'd be a guy who appreciated free countries."

The other went on looking at him with his mouth

clamped shut and his eyes hard with hate.

"I hope you know just what sort of a spot you're in," said the Saint carefully. "Kidnaping has been a federal rap for quite a while now, and I don't imagine you'd be very happy about having a lot of G-men move in on your life. On top of that, I catch you breaking in here—"

"I didn't break anything. The door was un- locked."

"That doesn't make any difference. And you know it. You were carrying concealed weapons—"

"Only because you say so."

"And just how do you explain being here?"

"I left a coupla books," Morgen said slowly. "I forgot them when I was packin'. I came back to get them."

"Why didn't you go to the house and ask for them?"

"I didn't want to make any trouble. I just thought I could find them and take them away."

Simon shook his head judicially.

"It's a lovely story, Karl. The FBI will have lots of fun with it."

"Go ahead. Tell them."

"Aren't you afraid they might be a little rough with you?"

"Why don't you turn me in and find out?"

"Because," said the Saint, "I want to talk to you myself first."

The man licked his lips, standing very stiffly and still holding on to the work-bench with big bony hands.

"I don't want to talk to you, bud."

"But you don't have any choice," Simon pointed out mildly. "And I've got a whole lot of questions I want answered. I want to know who gave you that note to put in my pocket at the Shoreham. I want to know who hired you to put the arm on Madeline Gray. I want to know who you're working for, in a general way. I want to know where Calvin Gray is right now."

"You better ask somebody who can tell you."

"And who's that?"

"I wouldn't know."

The Saint smiled very faintly.

"Tough guy, aren't you?"

"Maybe."

"So am I," Simon said, rather diffidently. "I'm sure you know who I am. And I expect you've heard about me before. I'm a pretty tough guy too, Karl. I could have quite a good time getting rough with you."

"Yeah? When do you start?"

"You don't want to play?"

"No, bud."

The smile didn't leave the Saint's lips.

"Bud," he said, "your dialogue is a little dull."

He put his weight on the foot that was on the floor, and followed it with the other.

He knew exactly what he was going to do, and he was perfectly calm about it. It wouldn't be pretty, but that wasn't his fault. He couldn't see anything handy to tie Morgen up with at the moment, and he couldn't afford to take any chances. The man really was tough, out of the down-to-bone fiber of him— and dangerous.

The Saint's expression was amiable and engaging, and he really felt that way, taking an audit of his good fortune. Only the icy blue of his eyes matched the part of his mind that was detached and passionless and without pity or friendliness.

He walked around the bench until he was within

arm's length of Morgen, and raised his right hand until his gun was at the level of Morgen's face. The other stared at it without blinking. Simon swung his wrist and forearm through a sudden arc that smashed the gun barrel against the side of the man's head. Morgen staggered and clung to the table. The Saint took another step towards him and jabbed the muzzle of the gun like a kicking piston into the region of his solar plexus. Morgen gasped throatily and sagged towards him.

The Saint took a half step back and slipped the automatic into his pocket. He used Morgen's chin like a punch-bag, giving him a left hook and then a right. The man let go the table and reeled back until he crashed into the wall behind him and slid down it to the floor.

"Get up," Simon said relentlessly. "This is only the beginning."

The man clawed himself up against the wall. He spat blood, and spat out an unprintable phrase after it.

Simon hit him again. Morgen's head caromed off his knuckles and thudded against the wall. The man's eyes were glazing, and only the same wall at his back held him upright. He stood flattened against it, his arms spread out a little to hold himself up.

"How does it feel to suffer for your Führer?" Simon asked gently.

He hit the man once more, not so hard, but stingingly.

It wasn't a magnificent performance, and it wasn't meant to be. It was simply and callously the mechanical process known in off-the-record police lore as softening up the opposition. But the Saint had no more compunction about it than he would have had about gaffing a shark. He was too sure of how Karl Morgen would have behaved if the positions had been reversed.

He was even more sure as he stared down Morgen's eyes, still unchangeably vicious and hate-filled in spite of their uncertain focus, but beginning to shift in sheer animal dread of such ruthless punishment.

"This can go on as long as you like, Karl," said the Saint, "and I won't mind it a bit. I can spend the rest of the day beating you to a pulp. And in between times we can try some new tricks with bunsen burners and some of the hungrier acids."

"You son of a bitch!"

"You won't get around me by flattering my mother. Do we talk or shall we go on playing?"

He poised his fist again; and for the first time Morgen flinched and raised one arm to cover his face.

"Well?" Simon prompted.

"What d'ya want to know?"

"That's better."

The Saint took out another cigarette and lighted it. He blew the first breath of smoke deliberately into Morgen's face. If he had to bully a bully, he could go all the way with it.

"Are you working for Imberline?" he asked.

"No."

"What were you doing with him last night?"

"I only just met him. I was tryin' to get a job with Consolidated Rubber."

"Why?"

"I want to eat."

"It seems to me," Simon observed, "that you're rather fond of rubber in your diet."

"You got me wrong, bud. I'm a chemist. I gotta

find a job I can do."

Simon's gaze was inclement and unimpressed.

"Who gave you that note to put in my pocket?"

"Somebody else."

"The same guy who hired you to snatch Madeline Gray?"

"That wasn't a snatch. We were just goin' to scare her a bit."

"I said, was it the same guy?"

"Yeah."

"Who?"

"Someone I work for."

"Karl," said the Saint genially, "I'm afraid you're stalling. Don't keep the suspense going too long, or I might get excited. Who are you working for?"

"A business man."

"Is his name Schicklgrüber?"

Morgen's eyes burned.

"No."

Simon smashed him on the mouth with a long straight left that bounced his head off the wall again.

"I told you I was excitable," he said equably. "And besides stalling, you're lying. I'm sure of that. Now tell me who else you're working for, and talk fast. Or else we are going to get really rough."

Morgen wiped his lips with the back of his hand.

"Okay, bud," he rasped. "Have it your way. We have got Calvin Gray. And if anything happens to me, it's gonna be just too bad about him."

"You've been seeing too many B pictures," said the Saint flintily. "That line is so standard that they put it in the script with a rubber stamp."

"You better ask Madeline and see what she thinks."

Simon didn't hesitate for an instant.

"I can't. She's in New York."

"Better ask her, just the same."

"I'd rather ask you. How much will it console you to think about what's going to happen to Calvin Gray while I'm broiling your feet and basting them with nitric acid?"

Morgen looked at him for quite a while, and that was one pause which the Saint didn't hurry. He let it sink in for all it was worth.

The man said: "Couldn't we make a deal?"

"It depends what the deal is."

"Gimme a cigarette, bud."

Simon backed off a couple of paces, dipped in his pocket, fingered out a cigarette, and tossed it over. Morgen fumbled the catch, and the cigarette flipped off his hands and fell towards the work-bench. He muttered something and went to pick it up. And then everything erupted.

Morgen was down on his hands, groping for the cigarette; and he must have been less groggy than he had let himself appear. Or else he was tougher than he boasted. Instead of straightening up, he dived forward like a sprinter off the mark. The dive took him right under the work-bench. Then the whole massive bench heaved up at one end as he rose under it. Glass slid and crashed on the floor; but Morgen was momentarily hidden, and the Saint had to sidestep fast and put up a hand to deflect the heavy table as it teetered over on to him like a gigantic club. He caught a blurred glimpse of Morgen plunging out through the hall, and squeezed the trigger of his automatic for a snap shot, but he was off balance and moving and it hadn't a chance.

The Saint's vocabulary, displayed to the right au-

dience, would have entitled him to a priority on ex-
communications.

He skidded around the upturned table and
darted through the hall in pursuit. Morgen was out
of sight when the Saint got outside, but the blun-
dering and crashing of his flight could be heard dis-
tinctly in the coppice to the left, and Simon's brain
was working like a comptometer now—when it was
a little late. Morgen—car keys—a car—the road . . .
Simon gave a second to clear mechanical thought,
and started down the path towards the house. Then
after a few yards he swerved off through a thin
space in the shrubbery to try and head off the retreat.

Something solid but soft intercepted his feet. He
spilled forward with his own momentum, and
sprawled headlong into an unsatisfactory cushion
and uncut grass. Half-winded, he rolled over and
sat up.

Then he saw what had tripped him.

It was a body which had been plainly exposed by
the encounter. Until recently, it had been inhabited
by the late Mr. Sylvester Angert.

4

The "late" was not to be taken too literally. It
wasn't so very late. The hands were still limp and
supple, and not particularly cold.

As for the instrument which had separated Mr.
Angert from his not very statuesquely modeled
clay, it was most probably the blackjack which Simon still had in his pocket. There was no blood on
Mr. Angert's clothes, no marks of strangulation on
his throat. His mousey face was relaxed, and he

didn't even seem to have struggled. But there was a depression in his skull just above and behind his right ear which yielded rather sickeningly to the Saint's exploring fingers. Apparently Mr. Angert's assimilation of calcium had failed to provide his cranium with the normal amount of resistance, or else Karl Morgen had underestimated his own strength. Simon had no doubt that it had been Morgen.

And Morgen was gone, now, and couldn't be asked any more questions.

The Saint used a few more time-honored Anglo-Saxon words in interesting combinations. Between the delay of the erupting work-bench, the delay of his fall, and the delay of finding out whether Sylvester Angert was an active obstruction or not, Morgen had stretched out too long a lead for the chase to offer many possibilities. Simon Templar raised himself to his feet, listening, and almost at once he heard the whirr of a starter, the grinding of gears, and the rising roar of an engine too far off to start him running again.

Then he heard something else—a patter of light feet running on the path he had just left. Instinctively he raised the gun he had never let go, and squirmed back into the shelter of the nearest bush. A moment later he saw the girl, and stepped out again.

"Simon!" she got out breathlessly. "Are you all right?"

"Fairly," he said. "I thought I told you to stay in the house."

"I know. But I was watching. I saw Karl running away—I was afraid something had happened to you —and . . ."

That was when she saw the body of the mousey

little man lying at his feet.

Her eyes widened, and then darkened with bewilderment.

"But—I was sure it was Karl—and it wasn't here—"

"It was Karl," said the Saint. "And he did run away. We were in the laboratory, and I was just getting around to a real heart-to-heart talk with him when he pulled a fast one. So I learnt a new trick." Simon twisted his lips wryly. "I was running after Karl when I fell over Sylvester."

Madeline Gray looked down at the motionless figure in rumpled clothes that didn't seem to belong to it any more.

"He looks sort of dead, doesn't he?" she said uncertainly.

"He is dead," said the Saint.

She swallowed something, and found her breath way down in her chest.

"You—killed him?"

"No. He was dead when I tumbled over him. He's been dead a little while, too. He must have been snooping around when Karl came here, and Karl thought he belonged to us and conked him— just a little too hard. So they weren't on the same side after all . . . This gets more interesting all the time."

"I'm glad you think so," she said, without any intention of being smart.

The Saint would scarcely have noticed if she had. His mind was busy with too many new adjustments, working resiliently ahead from the setback and trying to follow the sudden break in the pattern.

"Go on back to the house," he said, "and keep out of sight. I'll be with you in a minute."

He had already disturbed the body and its surroundings considerably by stumbling over it and then verifying its condition, so a little more disturbance would make no difference. Once again he turned out a set of pockets, and found nothing very extraordinary except the eavesdropping device which he had seen before. Mr. Angert apparently had been trustful enough to carry no weapons. There was a bulging wallet in one inside pocket, and a folded sheet of paper with a lot of cryptic scribbling on it in another. Simon replaced everything else, and took those two items with him.

He found Madeline Gray in the living-room, toying nervously with a cigarette.

"I don't seem to be much good at this, do I?" she said. "I'm frightened."

He smiled encouragement.

"You haven't screamed yet." He sat down beside the telephone. "Now I'm going to do something very dull. I'm going to have to call the FBI."

"I suppose that is the right thing to do."

"It's the only thing to do. I don't have a fingerprinting outfit with me, I don't have access to a lot of criminal records, I can't broadcast your father's description, and I haven't got an army of operatives to follow every lead. Aside from that, I'm wonderful."

He dialed the operator and asked for information, and after a few minutes he was through to New Haven.

"I want to talk to whoever's in charge there," he said. "The name is Simon Templar."

After a moment another voice said: "Yes, Mr. Templar?"

"Did you get a call from Washington about me?"

"Yes. Anything we can do?"

"I'm afraid I'm going to have to ask you to run

down to Stamford. This is a kidnaping. And incidentally there's another guy murdered, if that makes it sound better."

There was a brief digestive pause.

"Okay," said the voice matter-of-factly. "I can be there in about an hour. Where are you?"

Simon got the address from Madeline, repeated it, and hung up.

He lighted a cigarette, took out his automatic, and replenished the clip with a couple of loose shells from his pocket.

"So," she said, "it was Karl."

"It was. And he was also one of our playmates of last night. And he may have been the man who put that note in my pocket. I did get a few answers out of him, for what they're worth, before he foxed he."

He gave her a complete story of what had happened.

"I haven't any doubt that Karl is a Nazi," he said. "But somehow I don't think he's a big one. I don't know how big the Nazi angle is. It still doesn't look big—or else it's too big to see. But I'd be inclined to say that Karl was just put in here originally as a routine assignment, a sort of leg man, to find out what your father was up to. Did he have any chance to learn this formula?"

"No. Daddy never told anyone the real secret except me."

"I didn't think so. If Karl had known it, they wouldn't have needed to kidnap your father— which he admitted, by the way, when he was getting under my guard by pretending to break down —and Karl wouldn't have needed to come back here. I imagine he was sent back to see if he couldn't find some notes or clues."

"What else did he say?"

"He said he wasn't working for Imberline—yet. But I don't know whether I believe that or not."

"Could Imberline be a Nazi?"

"Anything is possible, in this goddam war. And yet, if he *is* a very brilliant and cunning guy, he certainly does an amazing job of hiding it . . . I don't know . . . At any rate, I'm sure that Karl is working for somebody else besides Schicklgrüber, even if it's only to cover his real boss and help him get into the places where he wants to be."

"Then who is it?"

"If I could tell you that, darling, I wouldn't be getting much of a headache. The new fun that we have to cope with is that the Ungodly don't all seem to be in one camp. Hence the sad fact that Comrade Angert's head will never ache again."

She winced at that.

"And we don't know anything about him at all," she said.

"No. But we may find out something now."

The Saint had his trophies on the table beside him. He turned to them to see if they were going to be any help, and the girl came over to sit on the arm of his chair and look over his shoulder.

He took the paper first. It was a plain quarto sheet, folded four times in one direction, the way many reporters use for taking notes. The jottings, after a little study, became much more intelligible than they had looked at first. There were the initials MG, the name Simon Templar written in full once, and the initials ST afterwards; there were places, figures which could be resolved into times, and an occasional item like "Cab, 85c."

"As we guessed anyway," said the Saint, "Sylvester was on your tail. And mine, too, after we met. He seems to have picked you up yesterday morning—at least, there are no notes before that."

He picked up the wallet next. It contained fifty-five dollars in bills, a deposit book from the Bowery Savings Bank with a record of fairly regular deposits and a final balance of $3127.48, a driving license, a couple of Western Union blanks, four airmail stamps, a 4-H draft card, a New York firearms permit, a snapshot of a young man in Air Corps uniform, a life-insurance receipt, a diary with nothing but a few names and addresses written in it, and a selection of visiting cards. The visiting cards were professionally interesting—Simon had a similar but even more extensive collection himself. They were designed to associate Mr. Angert with an assortment of enterprises that ranged from the Choctaw Pipe and Tube Company to the advertising department of Standard Magazines.

There were three cards, however, that the Saint stopped at. They said:

VAnderbilt 6-3850
SCHINDLER BUREAU OF INVESTIGATION 7 East 44th Street New York, N. Y.
Mr. Sylvester Angert

"This," said the Saint, "I can find out about."

"What's different about it?"

"It happens to be a real agency. One of the best. You remember I told you in Washington that I could hire you some guards if you wanted them? If you'd taken me up on it, I'd have passed you on to Ray Schindler . . . By God, Ray has a summer place near here, and there's just a chance—"

He was reaching for the telephone again without finishing the sentence.

He had that one stroke of luck, at least. He knew the voice that answered his ring without asking.

"Ray," he said, "this is Simon Templar."

"Well, well. Long time no see. How've you been?"

"Good enough. Listen, Ray, this is business. Do you happen to know a bird by the name of Sylvester Angert?"

There was a fractional pause.

"Yes. I know him."

"Does he work for you?"

"Sometimes."

"You're going to have to replace him," said the Saint cold-bloodedly. "Sylvester has gone to the Happy Sleuthing Grounds."

The wire hummed voicelessly for a second.

"What happened?"

"Somebody used his head for a drum and broke it."

"Where was this?"

"At Calvin Gray's place, just a little while ago. I found the body. He was following Madeline Gray, wasn't he?"

"Yes."

"And me too."

"I didn't know about that. If I'd known you knew her—" Schindler didn't go on. He said: "Have you called the police?"

"No. But I've got an FBI man coming down. There's more to this than just a murder."

"Just the same, if there's been a murder we'll have to notify the police."

"I suppose so. I'll call them."

"Better let me do it. I know the Chief. And I'll be right over."

"You know the place?"

"Yes. I'll see you in a few minutes."

Simon hung up.

"I'm afraid you're going to be hostess to a real convention of detectives," he said. "You'd better put a blue light outside and get out the cuspidors."

"You know this man Schindler," said the girl.

"I've known him for years. And whatever dirty work is going on, he isn't part of it. But anybody could have hired him to check up on you, on some pretext or other. I'm just hoping this will give us another lead. We'll see. Meanwhile—don't you think a drink would do you a bit of good?"

He went into the kitchen to organize a cocktail, and the girl followed him in there and watched him.

Presently she said: "You've been very sweet, trying to take everything out of my hands. But now, I've got to know. Do you think there's any chance of finding Daddy?"

"There's always a chance of anything," he replied, stirring his mixture methodically. "But this won't be easy. This is an awful quiet neck of the woods. Two or three men could easily come here, and pull a job, and get away again without ever being seen by anyone within miles of here."

Her eyes were stony and searching.

"If you're keeping anything back, I've got a right to know it. What do you think the truth is?"

He put down the shaker and faced her bluntly, and yet as kindly as he could.

"I think that I'm entirely responsible for whatever has happened to your father. I still don't know what makes it tick. But there's a pattern. Look.

You've had incidental sabotage and threats. They didn't stop you. Last night, I began to think that kidnaping your father, and the attempt to kidnap you, were a sort of co-ordinate maneuver—they could have been timed to happen about the same time, and you'd both have disappeared the same night, only in different places. But that doesn't work."

"Why?"

"The note you got in the Shoreham. '*Don't try to see Imberline.*' Your appointment with Imberline was a phony, a plant to take you to a place where you could be kidnaped. Therefore, why try to stop you keeping the appointment? Only for one reason. The Ungodly were still trying to weasel on their ungodliness. They still didn't want to go right in up to their ears. But you weren't scared off. You spoke to me. They told me to mind my own business, but they must have guessed even then that I wouldn't. They still might have thought they could put on some act and scare you off, but when I crashed on to the battlefield even that last hope was shot. At last they had to start really playing for keeps. You did all that when you dragged me in, and now it remains to be seen whether I can make it worth while." His lips set in a sardonic fighting line. "I'm sorry, kid, but at the moment that's how I think it is."

He was taking more blame than he need have, for it was obvious that a kidnaping of Calvin Gray could not have followed so quickly unless the plans had been laid in advance and there had been men waiting in the vicinity of Stamford who only needed a telephone call to set them in motion; but it made him feel better to take all the responsibility he could inflict on himself. It helped to build up a strength of cold anger that was some antidote to a groping helplessness which was not his fault.

But the girl didn't break. She said steadily: "Then you think they meant to leave me——"

"So that you'd play ball for fear of what might happen to your father. They weren't actually ready to tie you both up and work on you with hot irons. The threat and the war of nerves might have done the trick. Which is another thing that doesn't quite seem to fit the Nazi angle. And good heel heiler like Karl would have seen it the more straightforward way. But now—I don't know."

"Whatever it comes to," she said, "I'll be as tough as I can. I'm all right now. I promise."

He grinned, with one of his sudden carefree flashes of unreserving comradeship that could make people feel as if they had been elected to a unique and exclusive fraternity; and his hand rested briefly and lightly on her shoulder.

"You always were all right, Madeline," he said. "You just wanted a little time to find your feet in this racket."

He was impatient for the convoy that he was expecting to arrive. Even though he would be equally impatient with the routines that would have to be gone through, they would give a temporary air of positive action which he needed.

It was a long half-hour before the first car crunched into the driveway and Ray Schindler hauled his not inconsiderable bulk out of it. He had sparse white hair and mephistophelian black eyebrows and an amused inquisitive nose which gave him an absurdly appropriate resemblance to the late Edgar Wallace.

Simon went out to meet him, and they shook hands as another car drove in and disgorged a big ruddy man in loose tweeds with an ancient fedora tilted on the back of his head. Schindler introduced them.

"This is Chief Wayvern—Mr. Templar."

"Well," Wayvern said impersonally, "what's this all about?"

Simon told the complete story as briefly as he could, leaving out all speculation, while they walked to the place where the funny little man had so abruptly ceased to be funny. They stood and looked back at him in his final foolishness.

"That's Angert all right," Schindler said grimly.

Wayvern moved carefully to the body and made a superficial examination without disturbing it. Then he stepped back and turned to the two satellites who had trailed him with a load of equipment.

"Get started, boys," he said, "But don't move him until the doctor's seen him. He said he'd be here in a few minutes."

One of his men began to set up a camera, and Wayvern took a cigar out of his vest pocket and tilted his hat even further back.

"You say this man was working for you, Ray, keeping an eye on Madeline Gray?"

"That's right. He went to Washington the night before last to pick her up. But I didn't know about any of these other things that Simon has told you. This client who came to me said that Miss Gray had said that she was being blackmailed, and they wanted to help her. But Miss Gray had made this person promise not to tell the police. Coming to me was a dodge to get around that. At least, that was the story. I was commissioned to put a man on to watch Miss Gray and get a report on everyone who came in contact with her."

"Who was this client?" Simon asked.

"I called my office in New York to make sure of the name and address. Here it is."

Schindler took a piece of paper from his pocket and handed it to Wayvern.

"Miss Diana Barry," Wayvern said, reading off the paper.

"What did she look like?" asked the Saint.

"A big tall girl—beautiful figure—blonde—blue eyes—very well dressed and well spoken—"

Simon kept his face studiously blank, but he had been wondering how long it would be before Andrea Quennel crossed his path again.

4

How Simon Templar studied Biography, and Walter Devan came Visiting.

The FBI man from New Haven, whose name was Jetterick, said: "This Mrs. Cook says she served Mr. Gray's dinner at seven-thirty, and then she washed up and went home about nine. At that time he was reading a book in the living-room."

"He didn't say anything about going out," Madeline put in.

"No."

"Was there any reason why he should?" asked the Saint.

There wasn't any answer to that.

Simon had told his story two or three times over —the last time, for it to be laboriously taken down as a statement. Both of them had answered innumerable questions.

Madeline Gray had said: "I don't know anyone called Diana Barry, and I don't know anyone who fits that description. And I'm not being black-mailed."

Jetterick had phoned the description and address through to New York for investigation. A police doctor had seen Angert, confirmed the Saint's diagnosis subject to a postmortem, and gone away again. The remains of Sylvester Angert had gone away too, riding in a closed van which arrived later. Photographs had been taken, and fingerprints. The laboratory had been gone over with powders and magnifying glasses. Even then, men were working meticulously through the rest of the house.

"You're quite sure about Mrs. Cook?" Wayvern asked.

"Absolutely," Madeline said. "We've known her for years and years, and I don't think she's ever been out of Stamford. It won't take you a minute to find out all about her."

Jetterick rubbed his clean hard chin and said: "There haven't been any threats before, Miss Gray?"

"No. Only the notes in Washington, that we told you about."

"You said that your father was pretty well off, didn't you?"

"Yes."

"But so far there hasn't been any demand for ransom."

"Kidnaping for ransom," Simon mentioned, "doesn't tie in with two or three attempts to sabotage a laboratory."

"Was the sabotage proved? Were the local police told about it?"

"Of course," said the girl. "But they didn't find anything."

"We did what we could," Wayvern said.

"Accidents do happen in chemical laboratories, don't they?"

"Sometimes. But—"

"Didn't your father ever stay out at night, Miss Gray? You understand, I have to be very practical about this. According to you, he was under fifty. That isn't so old, in these days. I don't want to suggest anything that might offend you, but he hasn't been gone very long. Why shouldn't he have gone to New York—met some friends—decided to stay over in town—"

"You know as much as we do," said the Saint. "I've told you the whole story as I have it. You still have to account for the attempt to kidnap Miss Gray in Washington, the shot that was fired at me in the Shoreham, Karl Morgen prancing in and out of the picture, and the very dead Mr. Angert. But you take it your own way from here."

Jetterick looked at him with philosophical detachment.

"If it were anyone else but you," he said, "I'd have given you more trouble than I have. I admit you make it sound like a case. But I have to think of everything. I'm understaffed and overworked anyway. However, we are covering everything we can. We've got Morgen's description, and we'll get some of his fingerprints from the laboratory. We've got the gun you took from him to check on. We'll keep working on every clue there is."

"Isn't there anything I can do?" Madeline asked.

"Get me a photograph and give me a description of your father. We'll notify him as missing. If you do receive any communication about him, that'll give us something more to work on. Until then, I can't make any promises. There's a lot of space on this continent, and if a man is deliberately being hidden he can take a lot of finding."

The FBI man didn't mean to be unkind. He was just sticking to his job, and his textbooks hadn't encouraged the emotional approach to criminology. But Simon could see the girl stiffen herself to take it, and liked the way she did it. She hadn't just been making talk; she was all right now.

"I'll get you a picture," she said very evenly, and went out of the room.

Jetterick leafed over the notes he had taken.

Wayvern made another examination of Angert's wallet, which Simon had turned over. He picked out the snapshot of the young man in uniform, and shifted the long-dead stump of his cigar to the corner of his mouth.

"Know anything about this, Ray?"

"Yes," Schindler said. "That's his son. Or was, rather. He was killed in the Solomons."

"No chance of Angert having had any queer sympathies, then?" Jetterick suggested.

"Not in a million years," Schindler said with conviction. "He was crazy about that boy. Besides that, Angert worked for me on and off over a period of ten years, and I'd vouch for him anywhere. He was just caught in the middle, the same as I was."

"That's what it seems like," admitted Jetterick. "But I still don't get it. If Morgen was working for the same outfit as this woman who hired you, what would he kill Angert for?"

The same riddle had been distracting the Saint's attention for a long time; but he still kept silent about his ace in the hole. No doubt it was most reprehensible of him, but he had always been rather weak on the ethics of such matters. He had called in the FBI for their obvious usefulness, and the local police out of necessity; but he had no idea at all of retiring into the background of the case. On the contrary, he felt that his own activity was only just beginning. And Andrea Quennel was an angle to which he felt he had a special kind of proprietary claim.

Madeline Gray came back and said to the other three: "You'd better have some lunch with us while your men are finishing up."

They were drinking coffee when there was a phone call for Jetterick from New York. When he returned to the table his pleasantly commonplace face was stoical.

"They've checked on that address," he said. "It's just one of those accommodation places. The girl's description fits. But she didn't leave any forwarding address. She said she'd call in for messages."

"I could have guessed that," Schindler said, "as soon as I heard the rest of the story."

"We're watching the place, of course. If she goes there, we'll pick her up."

Simon drew on his cigarette.

"If she hears that Sylvester was cooled off," he remarked, "she isn't likely to go there."

"That's true. But we can try."

"Does she have to hear about it?" Schindler asked.

Jetterick shrugged.

"I don't have to say anything. How about you, Chief?"

"I'll do what I can to keep it quiet," Wayvern answered. "But I don't promise more than twenty-four hours. These things always leak out somehow. Then the reporters are on my neck, and I have to talk."

"Twenty-four hours are better than nothing," said Jetterick.

"While we're keeping things quiet," said the Saint, "I wish we could pretend that Madeline hasn't been here. The Ungodly are still looking for her. But Morgen didn't see her, so far as I know; and I told him she was in New York. Madeline can ask Mrs. Cook to stay overnight, and make up some story for her husband, so that there's no gossip around the town. The more we can keep Madeline hidden, the less likely we are to lose her."

"I can tell my men they didn't see her," said Wayvern.

"Besides that," Simon went on, "she ought to have a guard. Just in case. I've got to go to New York this afternoon, and I can't promise to be back tonight."

Jetterick grimaced.

"If I had a man to spare," he said, "I could divide him into six pieces and need all of them."

"I can take care of that," said Wayvern.

They all looked at each other. They seemed to have reached the end of what they could do.

"I'm driving in to New York," Schindler offered. "I can give you a lift, Simon."

It was still a while before they got away.

They talked the case to pieces all the way to the city, but the Saint was guilty of keeping most of his conclusions to himself and only contributing enough to sound natural and stay with the conversation. He had had enough analysing and theorising to last him for a long time. And now he was even more restless to get his hands on the dossiers that should be on their way to meet him. Somewhere in them, he hoped, there would be a key to at least one of the puzzles that was twisting through his brain. In spite of his friendship for Ray Schindler, he was glad when the ride was over and he could feel alone and unhampered again for whatever came next.

He was at the Roosevelt at four-thirty, and he was down to the last drop of a studiously nursed Martini when a thin gray man sat down at his table and laid a bulky envelope between them. Typed on the envelope was "Mr. Sebastian Tombs."

"From Hamilton," said the thin gray man dolefully.

"God bless him," said the Saint.

"I hope I didn't keep you waiting?"

"No. I was early." Simon signaled a waiter. "Have a drink."

"Thank you, no. I have ulcers."

"One dry Martini," said the Saint, and turned back to the thin gray man. "Did Hamilton give you a message too?"

"The party you asked about is staying at the Savoy Plaza tonight."

"Good."

"If you'll excuse me," said the thin gray man sadly, "I must go and keep some other appointments."

He got up and went grayly and wispily away, a perfect nonentity, perfectly enveloped in protective coloring, whom nobody would ever notice or remember—and perfect for his place in a machine of infinite complexity.

Simon weighed the package in his hand and teased the flap with his thumb while he tasted his second cocktail, but he decided against opening it there. At that hour, the place was getting too busy and noisy, filling up with business men intent on restoring themselves from the day's cares of commerce, and he wanted to concentrate single-mindedly on his reading.

He finished his drink more quickly than the last, but still with self-tantalising restraint, and put the envelope in his pocket and went out. His thoughts were working towards a quiet hotel room, a bottle of Peter Dawson, a bowl of ice, a pack of cigarettes, and a period of uninterrupted research. That may have been why he suddenly realised that he had been staring quite blankly at an open green convertible that swerved in to the curb towards him with a blonde blue-eyed goddess waving to him from behind the wheel.

He walked over to the car quite slowly, almost as though he were uncertain of the recognition; but he was absolutely certain, and it was as if the pit of his stomach dropped down below his belt and climbed up again.

"Hullo, Andrea," he said.

2

After the first chaotic instant he knew that this was only a coincidental encounter. No one except Hamilton and the thin gray courier could have told that he would be there at that moment—he had even let Schindler decant him at the Ritz-Carlton and walked over. But out of such coincidence grew the gambler's excitement of adventure. And there was no doubt any more that Andrea Quennel was adventure, no matter how dangerous.

Even if the only way she looked dangerous was the kind of way that had never given the Saint pause before.

She wore a soft creamy sweater that clung like suds to every curve of her upper sculpture, and her lips were full and inviting.

"Hullo," she said. "Surprised?"

"A little," he admitted mildly.

"We flew up this morning. Daddy had some business to attend to in New York, so I was going to Westport."

"What are you running on—bathtub gasoline?"

She laughed without a conscience, and pointed to the "T" sticker on the windshield.

"All our cars belong to Quenco now, and that's a defense industry . . . I was going to see if I could track you down in Stamford."

"That was nice."

She made a little face.

"Now you're stuck with me anyway. Get in, and you can buy me a drink somewhere."

He got in, and she let in the clutch and crept up to the light on Madison.

"Where would you like to take me?" she asked.

He had gone that far. He had picked up the dice, and now he might as well ride his own roll to the limit.

He said: "The Savoy Plaza."

He was watching her, but she didn't react with even a flicker of withdrawal. She made the right turn on Madison, and sent the convertible breezing north, weaving adroitly and complacently through the traffic, and keeping up a spillway of trivial chatter about some congressman who had been trying to date the hostess on the plane. The Saint was in practice by that time for interjecting the right agreeable noises. By the time they reached the Savoy Plaza he was cool and relaxed again, completely relaxed now, with a curious kind of patience that hadn't any immediate logical connection.

She berthed the car skillfully, and they went down into the cocktail lounge. He ordered drinks. She pulled off her gloves, giving the room the elaborately casual once-over of a woman who is quite well aware that every man in it has already taken a second look at her.

She said: "How are your protégés?"

"Fine."

"Did you leave Madeline in Stamford?"

As if he had only just said it, the recollection of what he had told her in Washington scorched across his mind; and he cursed himself without moving a muscle of his face. That was the one loophole which he had overlooked. Yet when he had created it, there had been no reason for not telling Andrea Quennel that he was taking Madeline back. It had seemed like ingenious tactics, even. A good deal had happened since then . . .

He said, as unhesitatingly as he had told the same lie before, but with less comfort in it: "I parked her with a friend in New York. I decided afterwards that too many accidents could happen on a lonely country estate."

"What about the Professor?"

"He's also been moved and hidden," said the Saint, most truthfully.

She looked at him steadily, simply listening to him, and her face was as unresponsive as a magazine cover. It was impossible to tell who was learning what or who was fooling who.

Their drinks came, and they toasted each other pleasantly. But the Saint had a queer fascinated feeling of lifting a sword instead of a glass, in the salute before a duel.

"You haven't found out any more yet?" she asked.

"Not much."

"When am I going to do something for you?"

"I don't know."

"You're terribly talkative."

He was conscious of his own curtness, and he said: "How long are you going to be at Westport?"

"Maybe not very long. We've got a place at Pinehurst, North Carolina, and Daddy wants to spend some time there as soon as he can get away. He wants me to go down and see that it's all opened up and ready." She turned the stem of her glass. "It's a lovely place—I wish you could see it."

"I wish I could."

"The gardens are gorgeous, and there's an enormous swimming pool that's more like a lake, and stables and horses. The riding's wonderful. Do you like to ride?"

"Very much."

"We could have a lot of fun if you came down with me. Just the two of us."

"Probably."

Her eyes were big and docile, asking you to write your own meaning in them.

"Why couldn't you?"

"I've got a job to do," he said.

"Is it that important?"

"Yes."

"I know it must be . . . But is it going on for ever?"

"I hope not."

"Mightn't it be over quite soon?"

"Yes," he said. "It might be over quite soon."

"Very soon?"

He nodded with an infinitesimal smile that was more inscrutable than complete expressionlessness.

"Yes," he said, "it might be very soon indeed."

"Then you must have been finding out things! Do you really know who all your villians are—what it's all about, and who's doing everything, and so on? I mean did you find your Axis agents or whoever they are?"

He lighted a cigarette and looked at her quite lazily.

"I've been rather slow up to now—I don't know what's been the matter with me," he confessed. "But I think I'm just coming out of the fog. You have these dull spells in detecting. It isn't all done by inspiration and rushing about, firing guns and leaping through windows. Sometimes a very plodding investigation of people's pasts, and present brings out much more interesting things. I think mine are going to be very interesting."

Her gaze went over his face for a little while; and her mouth looked soft in an absentminded way, or perhaps it was always like that.

She lighted a cigarette herself, and there was a silence that might have held nothing at all.

"Daddy's coming up to Westport tonight," she said.

"Oh, is he?" Every one of the Saint's inflections and expressions was urbane and easy; only the soaring away of his mind had left nothing but a shell of the forms and phrases.

"Why don't you drive up with me and have dinner, and you can meet him when he gets there? We can find you a bed, too."

"I'd love to. But I've got my job."

"Can't she take care of herself at all?"

"Not at the moment."

"Are you—more than professionally interested?"

He caught the flash in her words, but he didn't let it bring a spark back from him.

"I'm sorry," he smiled. "I just couldn't go to Westport tonight."

She said: "Daddy's very interested in you. I

broke down and told him about our talk last night. He thinks you're a pretty sensational person, and he's very anxious to meet you. He said he wanted to tell you something that he thinks you ought to know."

The Saint was aware of a fleeting touch of impalpable fingers on his spine.

"What was it about?"

"He didn't say. But he wanted me to be very sure and tell you. And he doesn't make much fuss about anything unless it's important."

"Then we'll certainly have to get together on it."

"What about tomorrow?"

"I don't know. Maybe."

"If you find you can get away," she said, "you've only got to call us. We don't dine till eight, and any time up till then . . . Will you do that?"

"Sure," he said, with just the right amount of politely meaningless promise."

"Let me give you our number in Westport."

He wrote it down.

"Your father isn't going home till late?" he said idly.

"No. He's got one of those awful business conferences. I'd have waited for him if I had anything to do." She pouted at her empty glass. "Why don't you get me another drink, sweetie?"

"I'm sorry."

He gave the order; and she sat back and reflected his gaze with blue eyes as pale and vacant as a clear spring sky.

"Are you staying in town tonight?" she asked.

"Yes."

"Where?"

"Here."

He had only just decided that, but it struck him

as a convenient step with a multitude of enticing possibilities.

She brightened her cigarette with a deep fretful inhalation.

"Why do you have to play so hard to get?" she demanded abruptly.

"I suppose I must be anti-social."

"I think you're wonderful."

"So do I. But maybe I have eccentric tastes."

"You don't like me."

"I don't really know you."

"You could do something about that."

It was quite plain to him that he could. It had been just as plain at their first meeting; but he hadn't given it any serious thought. Now he knew exactly why he had kept Andrea Quennel for his own special assignment, and what he had to do about it, because this was the part he had been cast for without even asking for it. Perhaps in a way he had known for several hours that it would come to this, without thinking about it, so that there was no shock when he had to realise that the time was there.

Two more dry Martinis arrived, and he raised his glass to the level of his mouth again; but this time he knew that it was a sword.

"Here's to crime," he said, and she smiled back.

"That sounds more like you."

Deliberately he let his eyes survey her again, and they did not stop at the neck. There wasn't a blush in her. She gave him back glance for glance, her red lips moist and parted. He let about half the calculated reserve soften out of his face.

"I told you I'd been a bit slow," he murmured. "Maybe I've been missing something."

"Want to reform?"

"It seems as if it might be more fun to degenerate."

"I could have fun watching you degenerate."

Then she pouted again.

"But," she said, "you're so frightfully busy . . ."

He knew just where he was going now, and he had no scruples about it. He was even going to enjoy it if he could.

"I've got some things that I must do," he said. "I can't get out of that. But I could get through a lot of them by eight o'clock. If you'd like to meet me then, we could nibble a hamburger and spend a few hours making up some lost time. Would that tempt you?"

"My resistance has been low ever since I met you," she said, and touched his hand with her fingers.

His mind was totally dispassionate, but there were human responses over which the mind held very nominal control. He was very much aware of the way her breathing lifted the roundness under her clinging sweater, and the eagerness that went out to him from her face. And he had a disturbing intuition, against all cynical argument, that her part in the game was no harder for her to play than his was for him.

Which was a good idea to forget quickly.

He said: "I'll have to get started if I'm not going to keep you waiting at eight o'clock. Let's meet at Louis-and-Armand's. We can fight out the rest of it over dinner."

"We won't fight," she said. "I'll chase around and see if I can find Daddy and tell him I'm not going straight home: And I'll see you at eight."

"I always seem to be giving you a sort of bum's rush," he remarked, "and here it is again."

She shook her head. She was suddenly very gay.

"Tonight is different, darling. Do you think it was Fate that made me see you outside the Roosevelt?"

"It could have been."

They drained their glasses while he waited for the check, and presently he took her outside and opened the door of her car for her. She got in and adjusted her skirt without any particular haste.

"I'll wait for you," she said. "You wouldn't stand me up, would you?"

"Not tonight, for a dictator's ransom," he answered lightly, and watched her drive away with the lines around his mouth smoothed in sober introspection.

He went back into the lobby, found a writing table, and enclosed a postcard announcing the forthcoming appearance of Larry Adler in an envelope which he addressed to Mr. Frank Imberline. He took the envelope over to the desk and put it down there, moving away at once and unnoticed behind the ample cover of the woman to whom the room clerk was talking. From the other side of the lobby he watched until the woman billowed off, and the clerk found the envelope, glanced at the name, time-stamped it, and put it in one of the pigeonholes behind him.

The Saint strolled back to the desk without taking his eyes off the pigeonhole until he could read the number on it. The number was 1013.

"Can you find me a room for tonight?" he asked. "Something about the tenth floor—I like to be fairly high up, but not too high.

He was about to register in the name of Sebastian Tombs, from nothing but automatic caution, when he remembered that Andrea Quennel might call him. He wrote his own name instead, and never guessed how he was to remember that decision.

After some discussion he settled for 1017, which seemed almost like divine intervention.

Having no luggage, he made a cash deposit, and went upstairs at once. He sent for ice and a bottle of Peter Dawson. By the time it came he already had his coat and tie off, and he was stretched out comfortably with his feet up, poring over the contents of Hamilton's envelope.

3

He took the report on Calvin Gray first, since it was the shortest. And it only amplified with dates and places the kind of picture which he had sketched by then for himself.

Old New England family. Graduated from Harvard, *magna cum laude*. Member of the faculty of Middlebury College, five years. Married; one daughter, Madeline, later B. Sc. at Columbia. Wife died in childbirth. Member of the faculty of Massachusetts Institute of Technology, nine years. Then a professorship at Harvard for six years. Inherited California gold mine at death of father. Check, check, and check. Retired, and devoted himself to private research. Author of one book, *Molecular Principles of Chemical Synthesis*, and sundry contributions to scientific journals. No political affiliation. A quiet modest man, well liked by the few people who got to know him.

Nothing much more than could have been found in *Who's Who*, if Calvin Gray had ever bothered to seek an entry there. But enough to confirm the Saint's information and his own final estimate.

He turned next to Walter Devan. He had recalled

a few associations of that name since their meeting, and he found them verified and extended.

Born in a small town in Indiana, father a carpenter. Ran away to Chicago at sixteen. News-boy, Postal Telegraph messenger, dishwasher, car washer. A few preliminary bouts as fall guy for rising middleweights. Professional football. A broken leg. Garage mechanic; night school. Machinist in an automobile factory in Detroit. Repair man in the Quenco plant at Cincinnati. Repair foreman. Then, in a series of rapid promotions, engineering manager, assistant plant superintendent at Mobile, personnel manager for the entire organization of the Quennel Chemical Corporation.

And that was where the biography became quite interesting, for Walter Devan's conception of personal management, which apparently had the approval of Quenco to the extent of raising his salary to an eventual high of $26,000 a year, was something new even in that comparatively youthful industry. He was credited with having become the field commander of Quennel's long and bitter fight against unionism, a miniature civil war which had only been ended by congressional legislation. He had been accused in a Senate investigation of instituting an elaborate system of spies and stoolpigeons, of coercing employees with threats and blackmail, of saying that any union organizers caught on Quenco property would be qualified for a free funeral at the corporation's expense. Certainly he had more than once imported regiments of strike-breakers, and been the generalissimo of pitched battles in which several lives had been lost. But he had easily cleared himself of one indictment for manslaughter, and the blackest mark on his legal record was an order to cease and desist. Entrenched behind his own taciturnity and protected by all the power of Quenco, he had become a semi-mythical bogey man, an intermittent subject for attacks by such writers as Westbrook Pegler, a name that the average public remembered without being quite sure why; but even if the papers in Simon's hands only collated facts and rumors which had already been found inadequate by the Law, they still solidified into a portrait which was realistic and three-dimensional to him.

It was, he meditated, a portrait that was well worth setting beside Walter Devan's very timely arrival on the scene of the attempted kidnaping, and the misunderstanding through which Morgen and his chunky companion had been enabled to make their getaway. Not to mention the Saint's impression that Devan could have been the man who squeezed by him in the cocktail lounge of the Shoreham, who could have slipped a note in his pocket if Morgen hadn't—but he wasn't sure about that.

The only thing missing was any special connection between Devan and Morgen. Devan, from his dossier, was no more concerned with politics than Calvin Gray. The only club he belonged to was the Elks. His only quoted utterances were on the subject of unions, and obvious sturdy platitudes about Capital and Labor, and, under examination, hardly less obvious defenses of the Quenco policy and methods. A pre-war attempt to link him with the German-American Bund had collapsed quite ridiculously. He was a man who worked at his job and kept his mouth shut, and didn't seem to divide his loyalty with anything else.

"And yet," Simon thought, "if he doesn't know more about at least some of this charade than I do, I will devote the rest of my life to curling the hair on eels."

He built himself another highball, and turned logically to the file summary on Hobart Quennel.

This was another of those superficially straightforward histories which any sound citizen is supposed to have. Quennel was the son of a respectable middle-class family in Mobile, Alabama. His father owned a prosperous drug store, in which Quennel worked after he left high school. Out of this ordinary origin, perhaps, in some deep-rooted way, might have stemmed both Quennel's ultimate aggrandisement of the chemical industry and his choice of Mobile for the establishment of one of Quenco's newest and largest plants.

Orphaned at twenty-one, Quennel had sold the drug store and gone north. He went to law school, graduated, joined a New York firm of corporation attorneys, worked hard and brilliantly, became a partner at twenty-eight. Married, and sired Andrea. Six years later, the deaths or retirements of the senior partners had made him the head of the firm. Two years later, he became the receiver in bankruptcy of an obscure manufacturing drug company in Cincinnati. One year from that, after a series of highly complicated transactions which had never been legally disputed, he was a majority stockholder and the firm was getting on its feet again. That was the beginning of the great Quennel Chemical Corporation.

The further developments were even more complicated in detail—in fact, Treasury experts had spent large sums of public money in efforts to unravel them—but fairly simple in outline. The obscure manufacturing drug company had prospered and grown until it was one of the most important in

the country. It had absorbed small competitors and
enlarged its interests. Somewhere quite early in the
tale, Mrs. Quennel, who had been an earnest art
student of Greenwich Village, found that her married life was unbearably deficient in romance, and
left for Reno with a Russian poet of excitingly
Bolshevist philosophy. Encouraged rather than discouraged, Hobart Quennel left his law business entirely to the junior partners he had taken, and devoted his legal genius exclusively to his own commercial interests. Over the following years, and out
of a maze of loans, liquidations, mergers, stock ex-
change manipulations, mortgages, flotations, and
holding companies. Quenco finally emerged—an
octopus with factories in four different states, no
longer concerned only with such simple products as
aspirin and lovable laxatives, but branching out into
all the fields of fertilisers, vitamins, synthetics, and
plastics, and presenting impeccable balance sheets
full of astronomical figures in which Mr. Quennel's
personal participation ran to millions of dollars a
year.

His present life was busy but well upholstered.
He kept the reins of Quenco firmly in his hands, but
found time to belong to a long list of golf, chess,
bridge, polo, and country clubs. For several years
before the war he had regularly taken a summer
vacation in Europe, accompanied by Andrea as
soon as she was old enough. He was one of those
Americans who once sang the praises of Mussolini
because he made the trains run on time. He had
rescued Andrea from three or four escapades which
had made news—one concerned with a Prussian
baron, one with the breaking of bottles over the
heads of gendarmes in the casino at Deauville, and
one with an accountant in Chicago whose wife had

old-fashioned idea about the sanctity of the home.
There was a note that several of Andrea's other
liaisons which had not become public scandals
seemed to have been impartially divided between
her father's business associates and business rivals.
Hobart Quennel himself was a model of genial good
behavior. He was a Shriner, staunch Republican,
and a dabbler in state and national politics. He also
had been the subject of a Senate investigation, a
defendant under the Sherman Act, and an implacable feudist of the Labor relations Board; but
with seasoned forensic skill he had managed to
emerge as nothing worse than a rugged individualist who had built up a great industry without
ever being accused of robbing hungry widows, who
was a diehard opponent of government in-
terference, and who had to be respected even if dis-
agreed with. Curiously, he had made public denun-
ciations of the America First Committee, and had
voluntarily pioneered in the compulsory fingerprinting of employees and in laying off all Axis na-
tionals even before there had been any official
moves in that direction.

"A deep guy," thought the Saint. "A very deep
guy indeed."

He had his own interpretation of some of the
items in Quennel's biography. He could see the
connection between the middle-class beginning
and the gigantic plant at Mobile, the local boy making good. He could see the link between the
Bolshevik poet and the Mussolini railroad sched-
ules. He could even tie up the bourgeois Southern
background with the advancement of Walter Devan as the Imperial Wizard of a strictly private Ku
Klux Klan. But all of that still didn't tarnish Hobart
Quennel's unimpeachable Americanism, misguided

as you might think it, or the fact that even the most
scurrilous attacks on him had never been able to
attach him adhesively to any subversive faction or
foreign-controlled activity.

Hobart Quennel was indisputably a very clever
man; but could he have been as clever as that, for so
many years, exposed all the time to any sniper who
wanted to load a gun for him?

The Saint lowered his drink an inch, and made
himself acknowledge that something he had been
looking for was still missing. And for the first time
he began to wonder whether he had been wrong
from the start. An easily preconceived idea, even a
series of very ready deductions, were desperately
tempting to coast on, and glutinously hard to shake
off once the ride had started. But facts were facts;
and the dossiers in his hands hadn't been compiled
by dewy-eyed romanticists. If Hobart Quennel had
even been more than essentially polite to any Nazi
or known fifth columnist, the slip would almost certainly have been recorded.

And yet . . .

Simon thought about Andrea Quennel again. She
had the build and beauty and coloring that Wagner
was probably dreaming of before the divas took
over. She might easily have been flattered by the
ideals of the Herrenvolk . . . There had been the
Prussian baron . . . And definitely she was the
Diana Barry who had commissioned Schindler . . .
If you disregarded the rules of legal evidence, her
own father had transparently taken advantage of
her glandular propensities before. In the same way
that she had been using them ever since the Saint
met her.

That was so much like the words she had used
herself that he could almost hear her saying them

again. He saw her life-like in front of him, her warm rich lips and the too-perfect contours of her body; and the remembrance was not helpful to dwell on.

He lighted a cigarette and picked up the last docket of the sheaf—the story of the man who was still the most nebulous personality of all.

Frank Imberline.

Born in New York's most expensive maternity home. A silver spoon case. Private school. Princeton. Colonial Club. Graduated *minima cum laude*, being much too busy for affairs of the higher intellect. Was then drafted by his father into the service of Consolidated Rubber. Served a six-year apprenticeship, being driven sluggishly through all the different departments of the business. Steadied down, acquired a stodgy and even pompous sense of responsibility, became an executive, a Rotarian, a member of the Akron Chamber of Commerce; eventually became Consolidated Rubber's head or figurehead. The latter seemed more probable, for there was a board of directors with plenty of shrewd experience behind them. The character estimate of Imberline said: "Generally considered honest and well-meaning, but dull." He played golf in the nineties, subscribed to all the good causes, and could always be depended on for a salvo of impressive and well-rounded cliches at any public dinner. His farthest traveling had been to Miami Beach. He had no labor battles, no quarrels with any Government bureaus. He did everything according to what it said in the book. His only political activity had been when some group persuaded him to run for Mayor on what was vaguely called a "reform ticket": he lost the election by a comfortable minority, and stated afterwards that politics were too confusing for him. Certainly the things

that Simon had heard him say made that sound
plausible. All the rest of his career—if such a swift-
sounding word could be applied to anything so
rutted and ponderous—had been devoted to Consolidated Rubber, from that early enforced apprenticeship until the time when he had resonantly
donated his services to the National Emergency.

And that was that.

Nothing else.

Not the barest hint of sharp practice, corruption,
chicanery, rebellion, conniving, strongarming, conspiracy, political ambition, or adventuring in social
philosophies. "Generally considered honest and
well-meaning, but dull . . ."

Of all the suspect records, his was the most open
and humdrum and unassailable.

Which turned everything inside out and upside
down.

The Saint lay back with his glass held between
his knees and blew chains of spaced smoke-rings towards the ceiling. Once again he put all the pieces
together, fitting and matching them against all the
facts that he had learned and memorised, estimating and analyzing with the utter impersonality
of a mathematician. And only getting back again
and again to the same irreconcilable equations.

He got up and freshened the melted ice in the
remains of his drink, and lighted another cigarette.
For several minutes he paced the room with
monotonous precision, up and down on one seam of
the carpet like a slow shutter in a machine.

He could cogitate his brain into a pretzel, but it
wouldn't advance him a single millimeter. He
would be in the same foredoomed position as an
Aristotelian philosopher trying to discover the nature of the universe with no other instrument than

pure and transcendent logic. But one renegade factor might be within a few yards of him at that moment, and if he left it untouched it would only be
his own fault that the solution didn't come out.

There had been moments like that in many of his
adventures—there nearly always seemed to be. Moments when the fragile swinging balance of thought
became a maddening pendulum that only physical
action would stop. And this was one of them. From
there on he was through with theories. He knew
what he knew, he had dissected all the arguments,
he had pinned down and anatomised all the ifs and
buts. He would never have to go back to them. The
solution and the answers were all there, if he could
beat them out of the raw material. The loose ends,
the contradictions, the gaps, would all merge and
blend and fill out and explain themselves as the
shape forged. But from there on, win or lose, right
or wrong, the rest was action.

He still had time before he had to meet Andrea.

He put on his tie, his holster, and his coat, and
left his room. He went a few yards down the corridor and knocked on the door of 1013.

4

Imberline was in his shirtsleeves, his waistcoat
unbottoned. He recognised the Saint in a surprised
and startled way that was too slow in maturing to
influence the course of events. Simon was inside the
door and closing it for him before he had decided
on his response.

"You'll begin to think this is a habit of mine,
Frank," said the Saint apologetically. "But honestly, I do make appointments when I have time."

"This is going too far," Imberline spluttered

belatedly. "I told you I'd see you and your—er—Miss Gray when I got back to Washington. I don't expect you to follow me all over the country. Even if it's a hotel, a man's house is his castle—"

"But needs must," said the Saint firmly, "when the devil drives."

He allowed Imberline to follow him into the room, and helped himself to the most inviting chair.

Imberline stood in front of him, bulging like a pouter pigeon.

"Young man, if you don't get out of here at once I'll pick up the telephone and have you thrown out."

"You can do that, of course. But I'll still have time to say what I want to say before the bouncers arrive. So why not just let me say it, and save a lot of commotion?"

The rubber rajah made the mistake of trying to find an answer to that one, and visibly wrestled himself to a standstill. He inflated himself another notch to try and distract attention from that.

"Well, what is it?" he barked.

"A few things have happened since last night," said the Saint. "I don't know what all of them add up to, but they do make it seem very probable that Calvin Gray's invention isn't a crackpot dream."

"The proof of the pudding is in the eating," Imberline pronounced sententiously. "We've already discussed that—"

"But that was before Calvin Gray was kidnaped."

Imberline had his mouth open for a retort before he fully realised what he was replying to.

He swallowed the unborn epigram, and groped for something else. It came out explosively enough, but the roar in his voice lacked its normal fullness.

"What's that?"

"Kidnaped."

"I didn't see anything about it in the papers."

"It's being kept as quiet as possible. So is the fact that a man was murdered during the return engagement this morning."

Imberline's jowls swelled.

"Mr. Templar, if this is some cock-and-bull story that you've concocted to try and stampede me, let me tell you—"

"You don't have to," said the Saint quietly. "If you want to confirm it, call the FBI in New Haven. Tell them you're interested on behalf of the WPB."

"Who was murdered?"

"A man named Angert, employed by Schindler, who was employed by some party unknown to trail Calvin Gray's daughter."

"I never heard of him."

"I'm afraid that doesn't make him any less dead."

Imberline glared at him with unreasonable indignation.

"This is a civilised country," he proclaimed. "We don't expect our system to be disrupted by violence and gangsterism. If there has been any official negligence—"

"Something ought to be done about it," Simon assented tiredly. "I know. Personally, I'm going to write to the President. What are you going to do?"

"What am I going to do?"

"Yes. You."

"What do you expect me to do? If your story is true, the proper authorities—"

"Of course, I'd forgotten the dear old Proper Authorities. But you were a Proper Authority who was supposed to find out what Calvin Gray had on the ball. And apparently some Improper Authority thinks a lot more of him than you did—so much that they're prepared to go to most violent and gangster lengths to put him on ice."

Imberline fumbled a handkerchief out of his trouser pocket and mopped his heavy face. He went over to another chair and made it groan with his weight.

"This is terrible," he said. "It's—it's shocking."

"It's all of that," said the Saint. "And it stinks for you."

"What do you mean?"

Simon slung one leg over the arm of his chair and settled deeper into it. He was no longer worried about being thrown out.

"Madeline Gray had an appointment with you last night," he said. "You'll remember I asked you about it. You said you didn't make it. But she thought she had it. And she was on her way to your house when there was an attempt to kidnap her—which I happened to louse up. But it was rather obvious that the appointment, phony or not, was planned to put her on the spot for kidnaping. If anyone wanted to jump to conclusions, they could make your position look slightly odd."

The other stiffened as if he had been goosed, and a tint of maroon crept into his complexion.

"Are you daring to insinuate—"

"I'm not insinuating anything. Frankie. I'm just telling you what any dumb cop would think of. Especially after you'd been so bull-headed about dodging Gray and his daughter. Almost as if you didn't want them to get a hearing."

"I told you, there is an established procedure—a well-planned system—"

"And there is Consolidated Rubber, which I hear

was rather late in climbing on the synthetic bandwagon."

Imberline drew himself up.

"Young man," he said, with indomitable dignity, "I have never made any secret of my views on the subject of synthetic rubber. If Nature had intended us to have synthetic rubber, she would have created it in the first place. But only God can make a tree. However," he conceded magnanimously, "in the present Emergency I have not been influenced by my personal opinions. My life has always been an open book. I am prepared to match my principles with any man's. If anyone wishes to impugn my honesty, I cannot prevent him, but I can assure you that he will live to eat his words."

Simon put a match to a cigarette and regarded him with unconcealable awe.

"Incredible," was the adjective which he had spontaneously tacked on Imberline in the Shoreham, without knowing anything about him or having heard more than two sentences of his dialogue. He couldn't improve on it now.

"You ought to be in a glass case," he said.

The pattern snapped into place. And once there, it was immovable. His ruthless eyes had held Imberline under a microscope for every instant of the interview, and they wouldn't have missed even the cobwebby shred of a frayed edge. Even less than in their first conversation, when he had been completely baffled. But there had been no such thing. The précis he had studied hadn't lied—as he should have known it couldn't. He had jabbed Imberline calculatingly with facts, information, insinuations, names and knowledge, without rattling him for a split second on any score except his own sonorous self-esteem. No cornered conspirator could ever have been that brilliant. Not even the dean of all professional hypocrites could have been so unpuncturable. Histrionic masterpieces like that were performed daily in detective stories; never in real life. And this was very much a time for realism, no matter what pet postulates went down in the crash.

"Frankie," said the Saint carefully, "I'm afraid I'm going to have to shake your foundations a bit. I'm beginning to wonder if you haven't been too much an open book for your own good."

"Honesty is the best policy—the only policy," insisted Imberline, putting a fine ring into his new coinage. Then suddenly he was a rather helpless and flabby man staring wistfully at a bottle and a syphon on the bureau. "I was going to have a drink when you came in," he said, as if he had been cheated.

"Fix me one while you're up," said the Saint congenially.

He let Imberline muddle through the mechanics of bartending, without moving until a glass was put into his hand.

Then he said, trying to walk the tight wire between candor and offense, between toughness and tact: "Let's face it. You are an honest man. But everyone you meet in this evil world may not be such an idealist as you are. You may have been a sucker for some people who needed a front man whose life was an open book."

"My associates," stated Imberline, "are business men of the highest standing—"

"And Sing Sing," drawled the Saint, "has several alumni and post-graduate students who got used to hearing the same things said about them."

"You're letting your imagination run away with

you. This dreadful coincidence—suppose I accept your statement that there has been foul play—"

"Let me ask you a couple of questions."

"What about?"

Simon absorbed from his drink and then from his cigarette.

"You said last night that Calvin Gray was a nut. Why?"

"That was on the basis of my information."

"You said that his invention had been investigated."

"It has been."

"Who by?"

"I told you—there is an established procedure. You probably haven't had much to do with modern business methods, but I can assure you that the best brains in the country have evolved a system of—"

"I just asked you: Who? What is the guy's name, where did you dig him up, and which side does he dress on?"

Imberline blinked, and then rubbed his rectangular wattled chin.

"If it's of any importance," he said, "I don't think Gray's case went through the regular channels. I'm trying to remember. No, perhaps it didn't. I think I was quite impressed with him at first, and the very same day I was in a position to mention Gray's claims to someone else who is one of the biggest men in that field. This expert told me that Professor Gray had already tried to sell him the same formula, and he had made exhaustive tests and established beyond any doubt that the whole thing was a fraud. So naturally, in order not to place any unnecessary burdens on our system of investigation—"

"You killed it then and there."

"In a manner of speaking."

"And then talked yourself into believing that it had been thoroughly investigated by your tame experts—"

"Mr. Templar," said Imberline crushingly, "my information in this case came from an expert whom my Department would be proud to employ if we could afford him. A self-made man, of course, but the most important figure in his field today."

"And what is his name?" inquired the Saint, with a little pulse beating behind his temples—"Joe Palooka?"

"Mr. Hobart Quennel, the President of Quenco."

Imberline said it somewhat as if he had been the toastmaster at a diplomatic banquet, and Quenco was a South American republic which recently decided to become a Good Neighbor.

The Saint's glass traveled very leisurely to his mouth again, and his cigarette visited there after it, while his amiably sardonic blue eyes surveyed the dollar-a-year deacon with unsubdued delight.

Another piece had clicked into its niche, and the threads were sorting out. Calvin Gray had been a shrewder diagnostician than Simon had given him credit for. In fact, Simon had to face the realisation that a great deal of the tangle had been woven out of his own refusal to accept the obvious. Too determinedly on the alert for tortuous scheming, he had only succeeded in snarling his own skein. Now he was finally cured, he hoped, and this—this lovely and luminous simplicity—could chart a straight course between way stations to the end.

"So Hobart Quennel was your authority," said the Saint dreamily. "And Quenco has two million dollars invested already in a plant that's laid out to use the old butadiene process."

Imberline snorted at him.

"Mr. Quennel is one of the most prominent industrialists in the country. I may not approve of his perpetual squabbles with some other Government departments, but in my own dealings with him he has always been most pleasant and co-operative. The mere suggestion that a man in his position would be prejudiced—"

"And yet," said the Saint, "I happened to meet his stooge, Walter Devan, in Washington; and Devan told me that Calvin Gray's formula looked very promising, but just didn't happen to be in their line. Not that it was fraud."

"Devan isn't a chemist."

"Neither is Quennel, except that he once worked in his father's drug store."

"He has the best advice that money can buy. Devan must have been misinformed."

"Why would Quennel misinform Devan?"

Imberline waved a large hand.

"I am not impertinent enough to pry into Mr. Quennel's private affairs. Doubtless he had his reasons. It could have been no concern of Devan's anyway. The cobbler should stick to his last."

"Devan said that in front of Madeline Gray. And it's much easier to believe that he was trying to cover up Quenco's interest in suppressing Gray's discovery."

"Nonsense. Of course he was trying to spare Miss Gray's feelings."

"Pollyanna," said the Saint bluntly, "why the hell won't you see that Quennel is playing you for a sucker?"

He had said the wrong thing, and he knew it immediately. Imberline bridled and bulged again, his heavy face darkening. He stood up and boomed.

"Young man, that is not only an impudent suggestion—it's scandalous. Mr. Quennel is the head of a great corporation. A man of his standing has a duty to the public almost like that of a trustee. A great deal of harm has been done by cheap and irresponsible attempts to discredit some of our outstanding industrial leaders. But there is still a thing as business ethics; and thank God, sir, while there are still men of the caliber that has made America what it is today—"

"Spare me the speech," said the Saint mildly. "I seem to have read it before somewhere."

"If you expect to impress me with these wild and scurrilous innuendoes—"

"All I'd like to know," Simon said patiently, "is what you propose to do about it."

"Do?" brayed Imberline.

He seemed to have a defensive repugnance to the suggestion that it was up to him to do something.

"Yes." Simon left one swallow in his glass, and stood up also. He kept the stout satrap spitted on a gaze of coldly challenging sapphire. "Don't forget that you could be made to look rather funny yourself on the basis I mentioned a little while ago."

Imberline's eyes narrowed down into beady stubbornness.

"I shall verify your statements, naturally. As a Public Servant, I am obliged to do that. If they have any truth in them—and I still haven't discarded the idea that the whole thing may be a fabrication of your own—there will of course by a thorough investigation. But I'm quite sure that there is some perfectly simple explanation."

"I'm quite sure there is," said the Saint. "Only you haven't seen it yet."

"Now will you get the hell out of here again? I have an engagement in a few minutes."

Simon nodded, and glanced at his watch. He emptied his glass and set it down.

"So have I, brother. So just remember what I'm going to do."

"Next time, you can make a proper appointment for it."

"I'm going to make an appointment," said the Saint. "With the FBI. Tomorrow. In the course of which I shall mention your name in connection with that Madeline Gray business, and your dropping of Calvin Gray on Hobart Quennel's say-so. So if you haven't taken some steps by that time, the Proper Authorities will want to know why." He dragged the last value out of his cigarette and crushed it out in the nearest ashtray. "I hope you will all have a bouncing reunion."

He closed the door very silently behind him; and as the elevator took him down he was cheered by the thought that he had been able to insert at least one lively bluebottle in the balm of the Ungodly. Frank Imberline might be the nearest thing to a well-schooled moron; he might fume and boom and cling dogmatically to all his platitudes; but a seed had been planted in his approximation of a mind, and if it ever got a root in there it would be as immovable as all his bigotries. The fatuous honesty, or honest fatuousness, which had made him such a perfect tool might boomerang in a most diverting way.

Simon Templar rolled the rare bouquet of the idea through his mind. He had certainly hoped to have something sensational out of Hamilton's reports to confront Imberline with; but this might be even better.

It was nearly eight o'clock, and he was hurried and preoccupied enough to stride past a couple of men who were entering the lobby without recognising one of them until his step was taking him past them. He almost stopped, and then went straight on out of the street, without looking round or being quite sure whether he had been recognised himself. But the monkey-wrench he had flipped into the machinery clattered more musically in his ears as he hailed a taxi. He knew that it would produce some disorder even sooner than he had hoped, and he thought he knew a little more about Hobart Quennel's business conference that night; for the man he had belatedly identified was Walter Devan.

5

How Andrea Quennel tried Everything, and Inspector Fernack also Did his Best.

Andrea Quennel cherished a crystal balloon of the last surviving cognac of Jules Robin, and said: "Where do we go from here?"

"That could be lots of places," said the Saint.

He felt durably sustained with two more cocktails, a bowl of the lobster bisque which only Louis and Armand make just that way, and a brochette of veal kidneys exuding just the right amount of plasma from the pores. He was icily sober, and yet he was recklessly ready for whatever was coming out of this.

"We might take in a good movie," he suggested through a drift of cigarette smoke.

"What—and catch one of those Falcon pictures with some body giving a bargain-basement imitation of you?"

He chuckled.

"All right. You call it. What's your favorite night club?"

"I'm sick to death of night clubs. Remember? I was Miss Glamor Girl of Nineteen-Something." Her generous mouth sulked. "Leave it to me, then. I know where we'll go."

The green convertible circled back to Fifth Avenue and purred north. The wind stirred in her ash blonde hair, and her hands were as light as the wind on the wheel. She looked pleased with herself in a private way.

Simon Templar was equally contented. He would have paid a regal fee for the privilege of listening to the business conference between Walter Devan and Frank Imberline, with the chance of having Hobart Quennel thrown in for good measure, and he wished he had had the forethought to appropriate the late Mr. Angert's ingenious aid to eavesdropping when the opportunity was there. But he hadn't; and the Savoy Plaza had not been considerate enough to architect itself with a convenient system of balconies for listening outside windows, as any hotel which had known it was going to be used in a story of this kind would assuredly have done. The Saint had to be philosophical about it. He couldn't be in two places at once either, and he could imagine much duller places than where he was now. He cupped his hands around the lighting of another cigarette and leaned back to enjoy the air and the ride. To him, there had always been a kind of simple excitement in the mere motion of driving through New York in an open car at night, the car like a speedboat skimming through the tall angular canyons, dwarfed even by limousines like sedate yachts, and busses like behemoths towering and roaring clumsily along the stream. It was an atavistic fantasy, like defying the elements in a flimsy tent; and it matched a mood that was no less primitive, and a duel that was no less real for all its lightness.

The Park fell open on their left, and they drifted along its banks for a few blocks before Andrea turned off into one of the eastern tributaries. She pulled up outside a house with an open door and a dimly lighted hallway.

"Well?" she said. "Want to come in?"

"I don't remember hearing about this club."

"It's rather exclusive."

He got out of the car, and she came around and took his left arm. She pressed close to him as they went up the steps, in an easy and spontaneous intimacy; and he felt the gun in his holster hard against his side.

"You are careful, aren't you?" she said with the faintest mockery.

He looked very innocent.

"Why?"

"Carrying a gun when you go out on a date with a girl."

"I never know who else I might meet."

She laughed, and pressed buttons in the self-service elevator. He smiled with her; and he was very careful, keeping his right hand free and clear and his coat open.

They stopped at the fifth floor, and stepped out on to an empty landing with the same subdued lighting as the hall. She went to a door with a letter on it, and opened it with a key from her bag.

"Will you walk into my parlor?" she said.

He walked in. It was one of those things that had to be done, like leaving a front-line trench in an advance, and he could only do it with his shooting hand loose and ready and his muscles alert and all her nerves and senses tuned to the last sensitive turn. It was an absurdly melodramatic feeling; like the time when he had let her into his suite in Washington; but there was no alternative to unchanging vigilance, and the good earth had provided innumerable graveyards for adventurers who had drowsed at the wrong time.

They were in an apartment, he saw as she found switches and turned on lights.

"This is quite a club," he remarked.

It was a nice and ordinarily furnished place. He strolled around on the most casual tour of inspection, but he managed to open all the doors and glance into all the closets that might have harbored unfriendly hosts.

"Like it?" she said.

"Very much," he replied. "I miss some of the dear old bloated Café Society faces, but not too badly."

"I keep it for when I have to stay in town. That phonograph thing over there has a bar in it, and there ought to be some good brandy. Take care of us, darling."

He opened the cabinet and brought over a bottle and two glasses, and poured for them both. She sat with her long shapely legs tucked under her on a divan behind the low table. He took an armchair facing her, and sniffed his glass guardedly. It had a fine aroma, but he only sipped it.

They gazed at each other thoughtfully.

"Did I forget to tell you about my etchings?" she asked.

His mouth stirred slightly.

"Maybe you did."

"You don't approve of the way I lured you up here."

"I think it was charming."

"Then why do you have to stay miles over there?"

"I was just waiting for your father to come bursting in with a shotgun and insist on your making an honest man out of me."

"You *are* careful, aren't you?" she said again.

"It's a bad habit I got into," he said.

She emptied her glass and pushed it towards him. He refilled it expressionlessly and set it back in front of her. She stared at him sullenly, nipping one thumbnail between her white front teeth. She looked very young, very spoiled, and distractingly accessible.

"Why do you hate me so much?" she demanded.

"I don't," he said pleasantly.

"I think I could hate you."

"I'm sorry."

"Damn it, I do hate you! What am I doing this for? I never run after men. They run after me. And I let them run and run. I'm not a bit interested in you, really. I can't even think why I let you talk me into having dinner with you tonight."

"Could it be for the same reason that I let you talk me into taking you out?"

Her eyes were big with the pale blank look that he had seen in them before.

"Now you're even making me shout at you," she complained. "Come over here, for Christ's sake. I won't bite you much."

She patted the divan next to her with an imperious hand. He shrugged, more with his lips and eyes than with his shoulders, and moved peaceably around the table.

She picked up the second taster of brandy, still watching him across the brim, and drained it with one quick decisive tilt.

Then suddenly her face was leaning into his face, and her mouth was searching for his, and it was a kiss that began and clung and demanded. He was still under it for a moment, but he couldn't always be still, and this was what he was there for anyway, and he took what it was, and his arms slipped around her, and he wanted it to be as good as it could be; but his mind stood aside and watched. And perhaps it didn't stand so far aside, because her lips were soft and yielding and taking and her breath was warm and sweet in his nostrils and her hair in his eyes and all the richness of her pressed against him and moulding hungrily against him; and he wasn't made out of wood even if he knew that he must be.

So after a long time he let her go, and he was much too sure that his pulses were running faster no matter what his mind did.

She looked smug and angry at the same time.

"You're excited, too, and you know it, which makes it four times worse," she said petulantly.

"I'm sorry," he murmured. "I always seem to be apologizing, but it isn't my fault, really."

"I hate you," she said broodingly.

She picked up the bottle, poured herself some more brandy, and put the bottle down again after an accusing glance at his glass.

"You aren't even polite enough to drown it in drink."

"I'm afraid you took my mind off that."

He absorbed half the glass while she finished hers.

"All you're concerned with is your damned mysteries," she said. "I think you're the most exciting thing that ever happened, but I can't make a mystery out of that. So you're all set to turn me down before we start. I suppose if I were some stupid little ingénue like Madeline Gray I wouldn't be able to fight you off."

He raised satirical eyebrows.

"Darling, you couldn't be jealous, could you?"

"Jealous? I'm just mad. I don't like being turned down. I must have done something wrong, and I want to know what it is. Damn it, I'm not going to fall for you."

"Now I am going to be careful."

"You won't even let me help you with this job you're working on. You told me once I might be able to do something for you one day, but you still haven't asked me. You won't even tell me anything."

"I can't tell you what I don't know."

"You know more than you've told me. But you keep me at arm's length all the time. Anyone would think you still thought I was an Axis agent, or whatever you said."

His pulses were all quiet again. This was what he was there for, too; and it couldn't wait forever. It was like fencing on a tightrope in the dark, with nothing to guide him but intuition and audacity and a sense of timing that had to balance on knife edges.

He said: "What about that German baron?"

"That frozen pain in the neck? He wasn't a Nazi. At least, I don't think so. But that was before the war anyway." Then her eyes turned back to him curiously. "How did you know about him?"

"I asked a few questions."

"What else did you find out about me?"

"I found out that you were quite often interested in people that your father has been interested in."

"Why shouldn't I be?"

"I didn't mean that kind of interest."

She poured herself another drink, but this time she only drank half of it at the first try. She put the glass down and gazed at it somberly.

"I help Daddy out sometimes," she said. "It's the least a girl can do, isn't it? And I have a lot of fun. I go to nice places and I hear some intelligent conversation. I can't live with young squirts and playboys all the time."

"After all," he agreed, "there are the Better Things in Life."

"You're still sneering at me. At least Daddy doesn't think I'm too dumb to help him."

He nodded.

"The one thing I've been wondering about is—doesn't he think you're too dumb, or does he think you're just dumb enough?"

Her eyes dwelt on him with that bafflingly vacant candor.

"I don't ask all those questions. What I don't know won't do me any harm, will it? And it isn't any of my business, especially if I have a good time. I don't want to be a genius. I just want you to pay some attention to me."

"Like you wanted me to pay some attention to you when your father sent you to talk to me at the Shoreham?"

"There wasn't any harm in that. He only wanted to know more about you and find out what you'd been doing."

"And what did he want you to find out tonight?" asked the Saint amiably.

His voice didn't have a point in it anywhere; it was the same gentle and faintly bantering sound that it had been all the time; but he was waiting.

She didn't try to escape his innocuous half-smiling glance. Her stare was blue and blind and limpid and babyishly sad.

"I told him all about our running into each other, of course, and what we talked about; and I said I was going to meet you for dinner. But this was all my own idea. I wish I did know what there was between you and Daddy. I don't think you like him any more than you like me."

"I've never met him, if you remember."

"If you had, you wouldn't be so suspicious. He said the nicest things about you."

"I love my public."

"You're impossible."

She took up her glass again and finished it, and made a grimace.

She said: "I don't know why I'm wasting my time. You aren't worth it. But you can't get away with this. You stink. And I'm going to get stinking. Make me some more brandy. I have to Go," she said abruptly.

She got up and went.

The Saint sat where he was and lighted a cigarette. He sat with it smouldering between his fingers. After a little while he lifted the brandy bottle and topped up her glass.

He faced it, that he didn't know whether he was getting everywhere or nowhere. There were factors that still didn't tie in. And he had to be as light with his foil as if he had been combing cobwebs. He could still be so irremediably wrong. He had been wrong about Imberline. He still didn't know whether one of his later passes had found any crevice. She could be dumb. How much would Quennel tell her? Or she could be brightly dumb, as she had said, asking no questions because they might only create problems. He didn't know how much the brandy would speak for her either. He was only sure that it could be a weapon on his side, if it was on any side.

He heard water running in the bathroom, and then a door opening, and then she was in the bedroom.

She was moving about in there for what seemed like a long time. He didn't turn his head. He took a very light sip from his glass. But there were no frightening effects. He had been making it last, cautiously; but he could be positive by now that there was nothing illegal creeping up from it.

He smoked meditatively. She didn't come back.

Then her voice reached him peevishly. "What about my drink?"

"Did you want it?"

"What do you think?"

He stood up, garnered the glass he had filled for her, and sauntered into the bedroom.

She lay in the big bed, her white shoulders clear of the covers, looking pleased with herself like a naughty child who is getting away with something. There was a dress and stockings and lacy intimacies scattered about the room, but he didn't have to total them up to deduce how naked she was. She had a naked expression on her beautifully empty face that had far more impact than the mere fact of nudity. It matched the mindless acquiescence of her big cornflower eyes—he had a name for that impenetrable enigma at last. He didn't have a name quite so facile for the disturbance that she was always on the verge of driving through all his casualness.

He knew that this was a deadline, and in an odd

way he was afraid of it, but he didn't let any of that escape from his control.

"I see you like to be comfortable," he drawled.

He carried her drink over to her. She took it out of his hand, and raised herself so that the sheets hung perilously from the galvanizing surge of her breasts. He sat on the side of the bed without staring at her.

"Tell me something," she insisted.

He waited while she put half an ounce of brandy away, drawing placidly on his cigarette and flicking ash on the carpet. Then he said, without any change of tone: "A friend of mine gave me a ride in from Stamford today. Name of Schindler. We were talking about you."

2

He must have been expecting more than he got.

She said: "Schindler? Oh, yes. The detective."

"He had a man watching Madeline Gray. Name of Angert. On some fairy-tale about her being blackmailed."

"That's right."

"Because you hired him."

After that it reached her. She sat up so that the covers were called on for a miracle that they were scarcely equal to.

"How did you know that?"

"I told you that I'd been asking questions," he said. "I was getting quite attached to Comrade Angert, so, naturally I was interested. The description of Miss Diana Barry could have fitted a lot of people in the world, but out of the people I knew were likely it could only have been you."

"You're frightfully clever, aren't you?" she said admiringly. "You're so perfectly like the Saint, it isn't fair."

He kept his gaze on her eyes.

"Did your father ask you to do that job for him?"

"Of course he did. Was that wrong of me? I mean, I didn't even know you then, so how could I know it would have anything to do with you?"

"Why did you call yourself Diana Barry?"

"I couldn't give my own name, could I? He'd probably have told Winchell or Walker or Sobol or somebody. Besides, Daddy likes to do things quietly."

"Quietly enough to cook up that phony blackmail story, apparently."

"We had to give some reason, stupid. Daddy was just interested in these tiresome Gray people, and he wanted to know more abut them. Just like he wanted to know more about you. He's awfully interested in all kinds of people." She drank some more brandy and scowled momentarily at the glass. "Now I suppose you're going to be sore because I didn't tell you all about it. Well, why should I tell you? I wouldn't even tell anyone else in the world that much. It's just what you do to me."

He thought it was time to take a little more of his drink.

"Well," he observed mildly, "I'm afraid Comrade Angert won't be much use to you any more."

"I suppose not, now that you know all about him. So why can't we talk about something more amusing?"

She wriggled a little, like a kitten asking to be stroked, and made a half-hearted attempt to pull the sheets around her bare satin back. The sheets were having a wonderful time.

Simon flipped some more ash on the floor and put his cigarette back to his mouth.

"I take it you haven't been back to that accommodation address for any Schindler reports lately."

"No. As a matter of fact, Daddy told me this evening that I shouldn't bother any more. He's found out all he wanted some other way, or something. So that's the end of it, isn't it?"

"I don't know," he said inflexibly. "But if you had been there this afternoon you wouldn't be here now."

"Why not?"

"Because you'd have been too busy talking to a lot of rude policemen."

Nothing could have been more naïve and unfrightened than her wide blue eyes.

"What for?"

"On account of Comrade Angert is now very busy snooping on angels," he said.

She had her glass at her lips when he said it, and she left it cleaned of the last drop when she lowered it. She held it on her knees without a tremor, and her reasons must have been different from his. Or were they? . . . That was the instant when he had to miss nothing; but there was nothing there. Nothing in her eyes or her face or her response. It was like punching a feather pillow. She had to be better than he was. Or he had to be wrong again—as wrong as he had been before. And he couldn't afford any more mistakes. He was fighting something that only gave way around him like a mire.

It went through his brain, like a comet, that the whole pointless death of Angert could still have no point.

Just an unfortunate error; one of those tripwires on which the best plans went agley, wherever that

was. Karl Morgen probably hadn't intended to kill
Angert anyhow. He had just hit too hard. He wasn't
the psychic type. He had simply been on his way to
the laboratory to see what he could find, and Sylvester Angert had been skulking in the bushes.
Therefore Sylvester Angert had been neutralized.
There had been no reason for Morgen to have recognised Angert. You could look for all kinds of complex explanations, but it could be as simple as that.
Nothing but a collision between the cogs of too
much efficiency. Just one of those things.

And that could be why Hobart Quennel had told
Andrea not to bother about Schindler any more—
because Morgen's report, through Devan, had already made the round trip, and he knew that that
was dangerous ground.

The Saint was making everything very easy for
himself. And he didn't know whether it was really
easy, or whether it was tougher and more elusive
than anything he had thought of before.

And his eyes were still on Andrea Quennel's face.

"What are you getting at?" she asked.

"Comrade Angert got himself bumped off."

She turned the glass in her hand, and rather deliberately dropped it over the edge of the bed on to
the carpet. It was more like her way of putting it
down.

"And so you think Daddy had something to do
with that," she said from a lost void.

The Saint didn't move.

"Andrea," he said, "if you want to make any
changes, this is the time to do it."

Her eyes swam on him. And then she lay back
and covered them with her hands. The sheets gave
up the effort of keeping in touch with her.

Simon looked at her for a while, thinking how dispassionate he was. Then he reached over to the bedside table to put his glass down and stub out his fragment of cigarette in the ashtray.

Then, like before, he was close to her, her arms were around his neck, and her lips were seeking for his and claiming them; and this was worse than before. But he had beaten it before, and he knew the strength of it, and now he was even more sure that he had to beat it. He tried being perfectly lifeless and still; but that didn't stop her, and it was too hard to go on with. He put his hands on her shoulders and held her down while he pushed himself away until he broke the circle of her arms.

"It's no use, Andrea," he said in a voice that he steadied almost to kindness. "You're only cheating yourself."

She stared up at him with that big blank hurt and hunger.

"I didn't have anything to do with that man being killed, if he was killed. It isn't my fault. And I'm sure it wasn't Daddy's fault, either."

"I'm not so sure. And you belong to him."

"I want to belong to you."

"You can't do both."

"I can't be against him. He's my father."

"That's why I'm saying goodnight." The Saint couldn't hold all that kindness. "You've told me what I wanted to know, and that's what I came here for."

She didn't recoil from that.

She said: "I think you're making all that up to scare me. I don't believe it. I can't."

"That's your choice."

"And now I suppose you're going to tell it all to the police."

"Eventually, and if it seems like a good idea—yes."

"Well, I didn't tell you anything. I won't admit a word of it. I made it all up, too. Just to keep you talking. They'll laugh at you—"

"I've been laughed at before."

"Simon," she whispered, "couldn't you just lie down and talk to me about it?"

He picked out another cigarette and lighted it with a hand that was perfectly steady now.

"No," he answered judiciously. "I couldn't. So this is goodnight."

"Where are you going?"

"Back to the hotel, probably, for a start."

"No," she said. "Please."

For the first time he had really caught her. Her face had a strained frightened look as she lifted herself on one elbow. He stood at the foot of the bed and thrust ruthlessly at the faltering of her guard.

"Why not?" he asked. "Is that another job you had to do for your father?—to keep me here when I ought to be somewhere else?"

"No," she said again. "This is just me. Please."

"I'm sorry," he said.

He started to turn away.

She said helplessly: "I happened to hear them talking . . ."

He turned again, and his eyes were level and remorseless.

"Who are 'they,' and what were 'they' talking about?"

"I don't know what it was about. I don't know! It was just something I happened to overhear. But I was afraid for you. I know you shouldn't go back to the hotel. That's why I wanted you here. I don't want you to go away. It isn't safe for you!"

"That's too bad," he said curtly. "But it doesn't work."

He started towards the door.

There was silence behind him for a moment, and then a wild flurry. He heard her bare feet on the rug; and then she was all around him, shameless and clinging and striving, pressing herself desperately against him with all her wanton temptations, her face reaching up to him and moist from her eyes.

"No, please, you mustn't—don't go!"

"Why?"

"I can't tell you. I don't know. I don't know anything. I just know you shouldn't. Darling, I love you. You've got me. You can stay here. Stay here all night. Stay with me. I'll tell Daddy I'm not going to drive him home. He can get a train. He won't mind. I won't say you're with me. I don't care. I want you here. Darling, darling."

He stood without moving, like a statue, keeping his hands away from her.

"And then," she was babbling, "in the morning, I'll fix breakfast for you, whatever you like best; and if you still want to go back to Connecticut you can drive up with me, the trains are horrible anyhow; and you can have dinner with us tomorrow night and really meet Daddy, and I know you'll get along as soon as you talk to him, you've got so much in common, and—"

It came over him like a wave, like a tide turning back, swamping and stifling him and dragging him down, and he had to strike out and fight it and be clear. He put his hands up and seized her wrists and tore them away from around his neck. He was spurred with an anger that blended his own uncertainty and her stupidity, or the reverse of both; and it was more than he could channel into the requisites of scheming and play. He threw her off him so roughly that the bed caught her behind the knees and she sat down foolishly, her liquid eyes still fastened on him and her hair a disordered cloud of spun honey around her face.

"Goodnight," he said, "and give Daddy my regards."

He went out, crossing the living-room quickly, and closing the door behind him on the landing.

He went down the stairs, not wanting to wait for the elevator, and out to the street. A taxi came by just as he emerged, and he caught it thankfully. They crawled past the green convertible as he said "The Savoy Plaza." It was like an escape.

It was an escape.

He had a momentary vision of her again, her face and her eyes, and the lovely symmetry and infinite promise of her; and he blotted it out in a sharp cloud of smoke.

The point was what he was escaping to.

No one had called him or asked for him at the hotel. He took his key and went up to the tenth floor, and approached his door with a queer tingling in his spine. His imagination whirled out wild pictures of booby traps, infernal machines with intricate wiring that fired guns when a key was put in the lock or started time fuses to mature when he was well into the room. But he couldn't immobilize himself with nightmares like that. He opened the door and went in, feeling a little suicidal and mildly surprised when he continued to live. Nothing happened suddenly with a loud noise. He examined his dubious refuge inch by inch. Everything was as he had left it, except that the night maid had been in and turned down the bed. The emptiness of the bathroom gave him his first smile. At least he didn't have to concern himself with such exotic refinements as cyanide in the tooth powder or curare on the edge of a razor blade. But it was much too easy to be killed, if anyone wanted it badly enough—as he knew only too well from both sides.

He set the night latch on the door and went back to peer out of the windows. The bare flat walls of the building extended safely around his outlook. There were none of those balconies that he had wished for before, and no thoughtfully planted fire escapes. Of course, a hook ladder could get up or a rope could get down; but either of those expedients would be risking an upward glance from the street. The Saint drew his head back from the rising grumble of traffic, lowered the sash to within a few inches of the sill, and balanced a glass and a couple of ashtrays precariously on top of it, which would give ample warning of any uninvited guests from that direction.

He went back to the table and mixed himself a highball. The ice in the pitcher had melted, but the water was still cold. He sipped the drink at his leisure. It tasted refreshing after the heavy brandy. The atmosphere was refreshing too, even with its thin keen bite of suspense, after the febrile maelstrom that he had just salvaged himself from.

He forced that recollection out of his head again.

If there was nothing here, where else wouldn't either Andrea or the Ungodly want him to be.

The only place he could think of was Stamford.

Late as it was, he made a phone call there. A male voice that he hadn't heard before answered.

"Miss Gray? She isn't here."

"This is Simon Templar," he said.

The voice said: "Oh."

There was a longish pause, and then her voice came on the line—a little sleepy and breathless, but perfectly natural and unforced.

"I just wanted to be sure you were all right," he said.

"Of course I am. Has anything happened?"

"Nothing worth telling, I'm afraid. Have you had any news?"

"No."

"Are you being well looked after?"

"Oh, yes. Mr. Wayvern left the nicest man here —he's as big as a house and his hobby is collecting butterflies."

"Good. Tell him to be sure and stay awake so he can go on adding to his collection."

She hesitated a moment.

"Why . . . are you—expecting anything?"

"I'm always expecting things. But don't worry. I just want to be sure he's taking his job seriously."

"Are you staying in New York tonight?"

"I guess I'll have to. It's probably a bit late for a train. Anyhow, remember the story I've been giving out is that you're in New York, so it'll look more convincing if I stay here. By the way, I'm at the Savoy. I hope they're cursing the joint already, wishing they could find out what name I've got you registered under."

There was another brief pause.

"Simon—do you think this'll go on very long?"

"No," he said, with an easy confidence that didn't have to match the expression she couldn't see. "Not very long. I think there'll be plenty of things moving tomorrow. And I'll keep in touch with you. Now go back to bed and try to forget it until breakfast.''

He opened a fresh pack of cigarettes after he had hung up, and paced the room as he had done hours before.

He was still in the dark, and he could only try to get some slim consolation out of the hope that the Ungodly were equally benighted. He wished he felt more assured about staying away from Stamford. But if he had really been hiding Madeline Gray in New York, the Ungodly would naturally expect him to stay close to her. In fact, they might have been watching him from any point in the evening in the hope that he would lead them to her. That might have been what Andrea Quennel was worried about. Or had she been worried? Had she staged a terrific performance to try and drive him into suspicion and from that into a false move? And how would the Ungodly think? If he had hurried off to Stamford, would they have credited him with trying most cunningly to lead them off on a false scent, and thereby have been convinced that Madeline Gray actually was in New York? Would they think that he would never be so reckless as to leave Madeline Gray in such an exposed position as Stamford; or would they think that was precisely what he wanted them to think? . . . It was a game of solitaire played with chameleon cards.

And yet with all that, as he always remembered, he never thought of the real danger.

He went to bed and slept eventually, since there was nothing else to do. It was ten o'clock when he woke up, and he knew that he had been tired from the night before. He showered and began to dress; and he was debating whether to get a shave before breakfast or have breakfast before the shave when his door trembled with an unnecessarily vigorous knocking.

He went and opened it, and raised his eyebrows involuntarily at a familiar face that he had not seen for some time.

"Why, Henry!" he exclaimed. "Fancy your finding me here."

The familiar figure filled the doorway with its shoulders.

"Fancy my not finding you here," retorted Inspector John Henry Fernack harshly. "Come out and tell me what you had against Imberline."

3

It all fell together in the Saint's brain like an exact measure of peanuts dropping into an envelope from an automatic packaging machine. It was so neat and final that he felt weirdly calm about it, not even dallying for a moment over the mechanism that made it happen.

He said on one emotionless note: "He's dead, is he?"

"You should ask me," Fernack replied sarcastically.

The Saint nodded.

"I shouldn't. You wouldn't be here if he was beefing about somebody stealing one of his cigars."

Fernack glowered at him implacably. There was a lot of history behind that glower. Aside from being part of a routine which has made this chronicler so popular with tax collectors everywhere, it was rooted in a long series of conflicts and collisions that all flooded back into Fernack's mind at such times as this. It was a hard life for him, as we must admit after all these years. Personally, he liked the Saint; in a peculiar way, he respected him; as an honest man, he had to admit that in a complete perspective the Saint had done far more for him than he had undone; and yet as a salaried custodian of the Law it seemed to Fernack that the Saint's appearance in any crime was a doomful guarantee of more strain and woe than any police-man should have been legitimately asked to bear. Besides which, even if he had never succeeded in compiling the mundane legal evidence, he knew to his own satisfaction that the Saint's methods had a light-hearted and even lethal disregard for lawful processes which it was always going to be his duty to try and prove: it would be a bitter triumph for him when he achieved it, and yet his consistent fail-ure was no less galling. It was, inevitably, a dilem-ma that couldn't help having the most corrosive ef-fects on any conscientious policeman's equanimity.

He said, with almost reflex bluster: "Maybe you'd like to have another look at him and see what sort of a job you did?"

"I would," said the Saint.

Along the corridor, two uniformed men were holding back a bunch of impatient reporters. An as-sistant manager, torn between retaining the goodwill of the press and avoiding undesirable publicity, twittered unhappily to and fro. One of the reporters yelled: "Hey, Fernack, d'you want a special edition all to yourself?" Another of them said: "Who's that guy with him?"

1013 seemed to be stocked full of busy toilers in plain clothes. A police photographer was packing up his equipment. Other specialists were working over the furniture with brushes and powder, wrap-ping exhibits, opening drawers and closets, picking up things and putting them down. It was a scene of prescribed antlike activity that the Saint seemed to have seen rather a lot of lately.

The body was on the bed, an amorphous mound suggestive of human shape under a sheet, like the first rough lumping of a clay model.

Fernack pulled the sheet back. Imberline looked as if he might have been asleep with his mouth open. But his eyes were half open too, showing only the whites. There was a folded towel under his head that showed red stains on it.

"What did he die of?" Simon asked.

"He fell down in the bathroom and beat his brains out on the floor," Fernack said. "Don't you remember?"

"Old age does things to your memory," Simon apologised. "Tell me all about it."

Fernack replaced the sheet.

"Imberline left a call for seven-thirty this morning. That was about twelve-thirty last night. His telephone didn't answer. They sent a housekeeper to check up. She looked in, didn't see him, and sent a maid in to do the room. The maid found him. His bed hadn't been slept in. He was in the bathroom, wearing everything except his coat, with his tie loosened and his collar unbuttoned—and dead."

The Saint had a picture of Imberline as he had seen him last, in what was apparently Imberline's home-life costume.

"So he fell down in the bathroom and broke his head," he said.

"Yeah. The back of his head was flattened to a pulp, and there was plenty of blood on the tiles. If you can fall down hard enough from where you stand to do that much damage to yourself, I'd like to see it."

"I'm afraid you would, Henry," said the Saint

sadly. "How long has he been dead?"

"You know we can't say that in minutes. But it was since last night. And he left his call after you came in. The telephone operator remembers that it was while you were still on your call to Stamford."

"So of course I did it, since I was in the building. Was there anything else?"

"He'd been entertaining someone since he was out to dinner. There was part of a bottle of Scotch and a couple of dirty glasses; but one of them was wiped so there were no fingerprints on it. There were ashes and cigarette and cigar ends."

"When did he come in?"

"About ten-thirty, as well as the desk clerk remembers."

"Was he alone?"

"The elevator girl says he didn't seem to be with anyone."

"So naturally he was with me, since you remember my old trick of becoming invisible."

Fernack turned a broad back on him and prowled, glaring at his subordinates. They were finishing their jobs and becoming a little vague. Fernack drove them out and shut the door on them. Simon lighted a cigarette and strolled around placidly.

Fernack faced him again with his rocky jaw set and his eyes hard and uncompromising.

"Now," he said heavily, "perhaps you'll tell me a few things."

"I'd be glad to," said the Saint obligingly.

"When I came to your room, you weren't at all surprised when I asked you about Imberline."

"I'm so used to you asking me extraordinary questions."

"You didn't even ask who he was."

"Why should I? I read the papers."

"You even knew that he'd been staying here."

"I didn't say so. But I wasn't going to fall over backwards if he was. It's a good place to stay. I even use it myself."

"And you knew that he smoked cigars."

"Several people do. I've heard that it's getting quite common."

The detective kept his hands down with a heroic effort.

"And on top of all that," he said, "you knew he was dead before I told you."

"You did tell me," said the Saint. "There's a special tone of voice you have that fairly screams homicide—particularly when you're hoping to send me to the chair for it. I've heard it so often that I can pick it out like a siren."

Fernack drew a deep labored breath.

"Now let me tell you what I think," he said crunchingly. "I think you know a hell of a lot too much about this. I think you're in plenty of trouble again—"

Simon blew an impudent smoke-ring straight at him.

"Henry," he said reasonably, "doesn't this dialogue remind you of something we've been through before?"

The detective swallowed.

"You're damn right it does! But this time—"

"This time it's going to be bigger and better. This time it's going to stick. This time you've got me. We've played that scene before too, but I don't like to bring that up. A guy has been rubbed out, and so I did it. Because everyone knows that I have an exclusive concession to do all the rubbing out that's done in New York."

"All you've got is a lot of smart answers—"

"To a lot of moronic questions. Imberline gets himself murdered here, and I'm handy, so why not convict me?"

"When it turned out to be a murder," Fernack said ponderously, "I had to check up on the other guests in the hotel. I came to your name, and there you were—practically next door. Now be smart about that!"

The Saint took a long draught of smoke and smiled at him with tolerant affection. He cast around for a chair and sat down with a ghost of a sigh.

"Henry," he said, "I'm just not smart any more. I wanted to murder Imberline, and I found out he was staying here and what room he was in, and I made quite a little fuss about getting a room as close to him as I could. I wasn't smart enough to just ride up in the elevator and give him the works and go away again. I had to move in on the job. I didn't want you to have a mystery on your hands—"

"Where were you last night?"

"Oh, I was out to dinner with a babe and then over at her apartment looking at her etchings, and whatever time the night clerk says I came in is probably about right. I didn't notice it exactly myself. I just wasn't smart enough to bother about an alibi. I bashed Imberline's head in; and even then I wasn't bright enough to get the hell out. I went to bed and went to sleep and waited for you to find me." Simon flipped over his hole card with a silent thanksgiving for the unconsidered decision that had dealt it into his hand. "I knew that wouldn't take you long, because I'd registered in my own name to make sure you wouldn't be put off by any aliases. I'm just not smart any more, Henry—that's all there is to it."

Fernack gloomed at him waveringly. It seemed that this also was part of a familiar scene. He was convinced that there was something wrong with it, as he always had been; but the trouble was that he could never put a finger on it. He only had an infuriating and dismal foreboding that he was going to find himself on the same lugubrious merry-go-round again.

"You're just too smart," he said suspiciously. "You're trying to sell me the same bill of goods—"

"I'm trying to show you what your evidence would sound like to a jury."

The detective rubbed his suffering gray hairs.

"Then what the hell do you know about this?" he demanded almost pleadingly.

"Now you're being rational, dear old bloodhound. So I'll let you into a secret. I did know Imberline was here, and I did come to see him—among other things."

Fernack jerked as if a hot needle had penetrated his gluteus maximus. The smouldering embers flared up in his eyes.

"Then you are trying to make a goat out of me!" he bawled. "You're giving me the same old baloney—"

The Saint groaned.

"You ought to take sedative pills," he said. "Your stomach must have ulcers like the craters on the moon. I'm trying to set you on the right track. I did come here to talk to Imberline; that's all. I didn't make much of a secret of it, either—long before you ever thought you'd be interested. So for anyone who wanted to ease him into his next transmigration, it could have been almost irresistible. I thought of everything else, and I was too dumb to think of that. Maybe I ought to go to the chair for it, but there's no law that says so." The Saint's face was like stone. "It would have been perfectly easy to do. Your murderer could even have come into the hotel with Imberline. They just didn't ride up on the same elevator. The guy suddenly leaves him in the lobby, and says he wants to buy a paper or say hullo to a friend or something, and he'll be right up. He takes the next car, chats for a while, waits till Imberline goes to the can, follows him, and flattens his skull on the floor. Then he waits and watches for me to come in, and when he's sure that I'm parked for the night he picks up the phone and leaves the morning call, just to prove that Imberline was alive then and try to make sure he'd be found before I was up. He had a very sound idea of the way a policeman would think, with all due respect, Henry."

The Saint's voice was light and soothing, but the detachment of his gaze was not part of any clairvoyant trance. He was only hanging words on to something that had long ago become concrete in his subconscious. He was thinking about very different things—that this must have been the trap that Andrea Quennel had tried too hard to keep him away from, and that she had looked like a sculpture in alabaster even when she toppled so foolishly on the bed, and that one day he would really be as clever as he tried to be.

Fernack was still clamping his jaw and struggling morosely to stare him down.

"That's all very fine," he persisted obstinately. "But coming from you—"

"Some of it might even be in evidence," said the Saint. "If Imberline made that morning call, his fingerprints would be on the telephone. Unless the telephone was wiped. The murderer wouldn't wipe the telephone unless he'd used it. Unless there were any other calls from this room after that—or are you ahead of me?"

Simon knew from the detective's face that he had rung a bell.

"I had thought of that," Fernack prevaricated valiantly. "But in that case, who *did* kill Imberline?"

"Probably some disgruntled manufacturer of coil-spring corsets who objected to having rubber released for making girdles."

Inspector Fernack's sensitive scrutiny started to become congested again.

"If you're amusing yourself, I'd rather go and laugh at a good funeral. Imberline was one of these Government men. I'm going to have all of Washington riding me as well as the Mayor. If you don't know anything, get the hell out of here."

"I might be able to put you in touch with the right people if you were more polite. But I'll have to make a call to New Haven."

"Go ahead."

Simon reached for the telephone.

He had no doubt that Fernack followed all the steps of his threading through Information and the FBI to Jetterick; and he didn't try to rush the machinery.

After a few minutes he had Jetterick on the wire.

"This is the Templar Corpse-Finding and Marching Club," he said. "How are things with you? . . . Much the same. I haven't been up long enough to check with Stamford yet—you haven't had any bad news from there? . . . Good. Nothing on Morgen yet, I suppose? . . . Mmm. One of those

uncooperative bastards. I didn't really think he'd
have a record—he wouldn't have been so much use
if he had . . . Well, what I called you for was to find
out whether a bureau bigwig by the name of Frank
Imberline tracked you down last night to find out if
there was any truth in what I'd told him about some
of the ramifications of our country picnic yesterday
. . . Oh, he did, did he? . . . That must have been
fun . . . No, I don't think I'd better tell you why. I'm
going to turn you over to Inspector John Henry
Fernack of the woodcraft constabulary down here—
a maestro of mystery who wants to put me in a
striped zoot suit. Tell him whatever you think
would be safe for his little pink ears."

He handed the phone over to Fernack and
strolled with his cigarette to the window, floating
evanescent blue wreaths against the pane and con-
templating the dubious rewards of unswerving but
unsophisticated righteousness.

4

He didn't know what story Jetterick would be
telling, and he didn't pay much attention. He imagined it would be pretty complete as Jetterick
knew it. The one lead that Jetterick didn't have,
aside from the later developments of the day
before, was the one that ran to Andrea Quennel and
through her to Hobart Quennel and Walter Devan
—Simon felt sure that Walter Devan himself was
the actual killer in this case. He couldn't see the
introduction of any more outside talent, and he
couldn't see Hobart Quennel personally engaged in
mayhem either. If Morgen had been traced to Devan, Jetterick would have had a pointer in that direction from another angle; but even that hadn't

happened. And the Saint had practically discounted Morgen altogether by then, except as an accessory: the man's Nazi affiliations might be another story, but they were not this one.

Simon Templar had met property dragons before, often enough to feel almost sentimental about the smell of paint and papier-mâché that came with them; but now he had a pellucid and vertiginous certainty that his quarry was darker and deadlier than any of those hackneyed horrors.

He couldn't have explained very succinctly why he kept the whole trail of Quenco to himself. He knew that that wasn't in line with the most earnest pleas of the Department of Justice—but Simon Templar had always had an indecorous disdain for such appeals. It might have been an incorrigible reversion to his old lawless habits, overriding the new rôle into which the fortunes of another war had conscripted him. It still wasn't because of Andrea's long rounded legs. It might have been because he knew in cold logic how flimsy his own evidence was, even flimsier than the gauze he had just made out of Fernack's case against him; because he knew that there were no statutory weapons to pierce that statutory armor of a man in Hobart Quennel's position, because in spite of his challenge to Andrea he knew how Fernack and even Jetterick would have laughed at him, because he was afraid of the morass of red tape that could tie him up until his own phantom sword was blunt . . . He didn't know, and he didn't think about it much.

He waited until Fernack's mostly monosyllabic conversation was finished. It took an unconscionable time, and he wondered whether it would be included in the bill charged to the late Frank

Imberline's estate. He couldn't see much to worry about in that; when he reviewed it; and his brow was serene and unfurrowed when he turned to look at the detective again.

Fernack's brow was a little damp, obviously from overwork, and he was starting to puzzle over the pages he had scrawled over in his notebook. But his manner was reluctantly different under its brittle shell.

He cleared his throat.

"There's just one thing nobody knows yet," he said. "Why did you come to New York today?"

"To get some dope on certain characters," said the Saint honestly. "The girl was one of those things—she drifted in later."

Fernack didn't even respond to that. It gave the Saint's rudimentary conscience a nice clean feeling.

"Why did you want to see Imberline?"

"I didn't know, when I checked in here. It depended on what I found out about him. When his record looked clear—as you'll find out when you get it—I thought I'd just beard him in his den and see if I could make sense with him. I couldn't make much at the time, but it seems he was at least impressed enough to verify me. Which may have been just too bad for him. Like me, he wasn't smart enough. He wasn't smart enough to keep his mouth shut."

"And you don't know who would have shut his mouth for him?"

"I don't know anything I'd want to have quoted now," said the Saint, as frankly as he could.

Fernack closed his book and put it away. Simon felt sorry for him.

"Well," said the detective dourly, "I expect you

were going somewhere. Go there."

"It's getting late for my breakfast. What about some lunch?"

"I'm going to have to say something to those goddamn reporters."

"Next time, then."

"I hope that won't be for another fifty years."

"It's too bad, Henry," said the Saint with almost genuine sympathy. "This is going to be a hell of a case for you—what with the complications of the FBI and another link in the next state. But that's what the Proper Authorities have badges for."

He went back to his own room.

He finished dressing with his tie and coat, picked up the remains of his ruminative bottle of Peter Dawson, and started back towards the elevators. Inevitably, a loitering cub, detailed to guard the flank, intercepted him before he got there.

"Mr. Templar, may I ask you a question?"

"Ask me anything you like," said the Saint liberally. "I'm just a perambulating ouija board."

"Are you helping the police in this case, or are they trying to pin something on you?"

Simon deposited the bottle carefully in his hands.

"The whole solution of the mystery," he said, "is probably contained in this sample of the saliva of a dromedary which was found eating the stuffing out of Imberline's mattress. And if you want the truth," he added hollowly, "Naval Intelligence has a theory that Fernack himself poisoned both of them."

The assistant manager twittering still more anxiously, created enough diversion for the Saint to catch a descending car and make a solitary exit.

Simon regulated his bill at the desk with sublime sangfroid, since it was a most ethical hermitage, and he might want to use it again, and it was no fault of the management if careless guests asked to be slaughtered in its upper regions, and left its portals without a smudge on his credit rating or any visible objection to the cloud of sleuths who might have been following him like a smokescreen of bees on the scent of the last wilting clover blossom of the season.

He went to Grand Central, enjoyed a shave at the Terminal Barber Shop, and was driven from there by the pangs of purely prosaic hunger to the Oyster Bar, where he took his time over the massacre of several inoffensive molluscs. It was after lunch that he became highly inconsiderate of the convenience of possible shadows. His method, which need not be followed in detail, involved some tricky work around subway turnstiles, some fast zigzagging in the Commodore Hotel, and a short excursion through a corner drug store; and when he re-entered Grand Central through the Biltmore tunnel he was quite sure that he would have shaken off anyone who wasn't attached to him with a rope. He found a train leaving for Stamford in five minutes, stopped to buy a newspaper, and settled in with it.

The paper called itself an Extra, but the only thing extra about it was the size of the headlines. They said RUBBER DIRECTOR MURDERED, and that was approximately what the story consisted of. The city editor had done his best to give it a big lead with a lot of "Mystery surrounds" and "It is suspecteds," but his reporter had been able to put very few bones into it at that point. A prefabricated sketch of Frank Imberline's life and career ran alongside under a double-column head and tried to make the story look good.

Simon glanced through the war news, the comics,

and the baseball scores, and put the paper down.

He wondered what story Fernack would give out when they cornered him. He wondered whether he should have asked Jetterick to ask Fernack to keep any connection with the Angert murder and the Gray kidnaping out of it, or whether Jetterick would have done that on his own. He decided that this was probably unnecessary wondering. There wasn't any real need to bring those links in, except to give a bigger splash to the case; and Fernack wasn't the type of officer who went in for that.

He opened the paper again, on a second thought, and went through it item by item to find out whether anything about Angert and/or Gray had been printed and pushed into obscurity by the big local break; but there wasn't a word. Jetterick and Wayvern had been able to achieve that much anyhow. But how much longer they would be able to keep it up was extremely problematical.

Then he decided that that wouldn't matter much longer. The Ungodly might have been misled for a while; but sooner or later, if they were as efficient as he thought they were, they would investigate Stamford again, just for luck. But he might have gained several hours, which had made his trip to New York easier; and now he was on his way back to Madeline. Now they could find her there, and he would be looking forward to it.

He checked the new disposition again in his mind.

The Ungodly would know now that the heat was on for keeps. They would have been afraid of it from Morgen's story, and even more perturbed when Andrea Quennel reported that the Saint was staying at the Savoy Plaza—where Imberline was. They would have had no more doubt after they spoke to Imberline. That was how Imberline earned his obituary. But they had hoped to break out of the web by throwing suspicion on to the Saint with the inviting circumstances which must have seemed ready-made for them. Now, very soon now, through a newspaper or otherwise, they would learn that Simon Templar had been questioned by the police and released. They would know that something had gone wrong again. And they would know that they had very little time.

Then it was all a balance of imponderables again.

How much would they think the Saint had told? How much, for that matter, did they believe the Saint knew?

Simon couldn't hazard the second question. It depended a little, perhaps not too much, on Andrea's version of the previous night. And that was something that it was impossible to guess, for many reasons.

But they would be afraid that the Saint knew something. And he hoped that they would be good enough psychologists to figure that he would keep the best of it to himself. He thought they would. He was gambling more than he cared to measure on that.

They had to argue that if he knew too much he knew that they had Calvin Gray. Therefore his object would be to recover that hostage. He, on the other hand, had Madeline Gray, who was just as important. Each of them held one trump at par. It was a deadlock. The only difference was that they could threaten to do vicious things to Calvin Gray, and be wholly unmoved even if the Saint fantastically threatened reprisals on Madeline. But they could well doubt whether in the last extremity even the Saint would let himself be intimidated by that. Therefore, before the game could end, one side would have to hold both trumps. The difference there was that the Saint could wait; he had a minuscule advantage in time. They hadn't.

Simon hoped that was how it was.

He had nothing to do but play chords on that until the train stopped at Stamford.

He secured a taxi in company with a young sergeant on furlough and a stout woman with three Siamese cats in a wicker basket who must ineluctably have been some hapless individual's visiting aunt, and began to fume inwardly for the first time while they were dropped off at nearer destinations. After that, it seemed almost like another superfluous delay when he recognized Wayvern and another man in a dark sedan that met and passed them out on Long Ridge Road. But Wayvern recognized him at the same time, so the Saint stopped his driver, and the two cars slowed down a few yards past each other and backed up until they could talk.

"What goes?" Simon asked.

"I was just taking my man home," Wayvern told him. "Jetterick phoned me and said it was all clear now."

"And about time," said the collector of butterflies, yawning. "I ain't had a night's sleep since Christmas."

The Saint didn't know why the earth seemed to stand still.

"Where've you been?" Wayvern asked him.

"On a train coming back from New York."

"Then I guess he couldn't get in touch with you. Better phone him." Wayvern put his car in gear again and stirred the engine. "He said he might be coming over. If I see him first, I'll tell him you're back."

Simon nodded, and told his driver to go on.

He could give no reason for it, and certainly there was nothing he could have said to Wayvern, but his premonition was so sure that it was like extrasensory knowledge. It sat just below his ribs with a leaden dullness that made the plodding taxi seem even slower. He insulted himself in a quiet monotonous way; but that did no good except to pass the time. What had happened couldn't be altered. And he knew what had happened, so positively, so inevitably, that when he went into the house and called Madeline, and she didn't answer, it wasn't a shock or an impact at all, but only a sort of draining at his diaphragm, as if he had been hit in the solar plexus without feeling the actual blow.

It was Mrs. Cook who came out of the kitchen while he was calling, and said: "I think Miss Gray went out."

"What do you mean, you think she went out?" Simon asked with icy impassivity.

"Well, after Mr. Wayvern took his man away, I heard her saying goodbye to them, and presently there was another car drove up and I think she went out. I'd heard them saying that everything was all right, and she was very excited. I thought perhaps you'd come back for her."

"You didn't see this other car, or anyone else who came here?"

"No, sir." He had gathered that morning that she was an optimistic creature with a happily vacant mind, but even she must have felt something in his stillness and the coldness of his voice. "Why—is anything wrong?"

There was nothing that Simon could see any use in discussing with her.

"No."

He turned on his heel and went into the living-room, and for some minutes he stood rigidly there before he began to pace. He had exactly the same feeling, differently polarized, that an amateur criminal must have who has committed his first defalcation and then realized that he has made a fatal slip and that he must be found out and that it will only be a matter of time before they come for him, that he has changed the whole course of his life in a blithe moment and now the machinery has got him and there is nothing he can do about it. It wasn't like that for the Saint, but it felt the same.

He didn't even bother about calling Jetterick for a double check. He didn't need that melancholy confirmation. He knew.

As for calling Jetterick or Wayvern to make them do something—that was just dreamy thinking. That would mean starting all over again. And there was nothing more to start with than there had been before, when Calvin Gray vanished. You could have all the microscopes and all the organization on earth, but you couldn't do much if nobody had seen anyone and nothing was left behind and there was nothing to start with. Not for a long time, anyway. And that might be much too long.

And under the handicaps of democratic justice, you couldn't make inspirational forays in all directions in the hope of blasting out something that would justify them. You couldn't take the bare word and extravagant theories even of a Saint as a sound basis for hurling reckless charges against a man with the power and prominence of Hobart Quennel. Because if you were pulling a boner it would be just too damn bad about you.

Unless your name happened to be Simon

Templar, the Saint, and you never had given a damn.

Simon thought all that out, and hammered the shape of it into his mind.

The Ungodly had thought it out, too. Just as he'd hoped they would. But sooner.

And now he was an outlaw again, nothing else; and any riposte he made could only be in his own way.

It was five o'clock when he called Westport.

He wondered if she would be there. But she was. Her voice answered the ring, as if she had been expecting it. She might have been expecting it, too. He could take that in his stride, now, with everything else. He was on his own now, regardless of Hamilton or anyone. And all the hell-for-leather brigand lilt of the old days was rousing in his voice and edging into the piratical hardening of his blue eyes as he greeted her.

"Andrea," he said. "Thanks. For everything. And I decided to take you up on that invitation. I'll be over for dinner."

6

How Hobart Quennel discoursed about Business, and Calvin Gray did what the Saint told Him.

Mr. Hobart Quennel looked no more like a millionaire than any other millionaire; and probably he was just as secretly proud of the fact as any other up-to-date millionare. He was one of hundreds of modern refutations of the old crude Communist caricatures of a capitalist, so that Simon Templar wondered whether there might be some congenital instinct of camouflage in the cosmogony of millionaires which caused them as a race to keep one jump ahead of their unpopular prototypes. It was, as if in these days of ruthless social consciousness a millionaire required some kind of protective coloration to enable him to succeed in his déclassé profession.

Mr. Quennel was physically a fairly big and well-built man, with his daughter's fair hair sprinkled with gray and balding back from his forehead, and the same pale blue inexpressive eyes. But he gave no impression of being either frightening or furtive, for in these days of higher education it is no longer so easy as it may once have been to bludgeon the crisp cabbage out of the public purse, and a man who looks either frightening or furtive has too many strikes against him when he bids for the big bullion. His face was smooth and bony without being cadaverous, so that its fundamental hardness was calm and without strain. His clothes were good when you noticed them, but it was just as easy not to notice them at all. He had no softening around the middle, for that mode is also out of fashion among millionaires, who are conspicuous among sedentary workers for being able to afford all the trainers and masseurs and golf clubs and other exercising appliances that can be prescribed to restrain the middle-age equator. He was that new and fascinating evolution of the primitive tycoon who simply worked at the job of being a millionaire, as unexcitedly as other men worked at the job of being bricklayers, and probably with no more grandiose ideas of his place in the engine of civilisation. It was just a job in which you weighed different factors and did different things in different ways, and you had a different wage scale and standard of living; but then bricklayers were different again from cowboys, but they didn't confuse their personal reactions by thinking about cowboys.

He shook hands with the Saint, and said "I'm very glad to meet you," and personally poured Martinis from the shaker he had been stirring.

He had a pleasant voice and manner, dignified but cordial, neither ingratiating nor domineering. He had the soothing confidence of a man who didn't need to ask favors, or to go out of his way to offer them. He was a guy you could like. Simon

Templar liked him in his own way, and felt just as comfortable. He sat down on the sofa beside Andrea Quennel, and crossed his long legs, and said: "This is quite a place you have here."

"Like it?" She sounded as if she wanted it to be liked, as if it were a new dress. "But I think you'd like Pinehurst much more. I do. It's more sort of outdoorsy."

She looked as sort of outdoorsy as an orchid. She wore one of those house-coat-dinner-dress effects that would get by anywhere between a ballroom and a boudoir and still always have a faint air of belonging somewhere else. It had a high strapped Grecian bodice line that did sensational things for her sensational torso. She had opened the door when he arrived, and it had seemed to him that her classic face, and melting receptive mouth were like candy in a confectioner's window, lovely and desirable but without volition. He knew now that this was a fault of his own perception, but he was still inching his way through the third dimension that had to bring the whole picture into sudden life and clarity.

It felt a little unearthly to be meeting her like that, in this atmosphere of ordinary and pleasant formality, after the way they had last seen each other. He wondered what she was thinking. But he had been able to read nothing in her face, not even embarrassment; and they hadn't been alone together for a moment. He didn't know whether to be glad of that or not. They watched each other inscrutably, like a pair of cats at opposite ends of a wall.

There was one other person who had to be there to complete the pattern, and a few minutes later he came in, looking very much freshly scrubbed and brushed, in a plain blue suit that was a little tight around the chest and biceps, so that he had some of the air of a stevedore dressed up in his Sunday best. Mr. Quennel patted him on the shoulder and said: "Hullo, Walter . . . You've met Mr. Templar, haven't you?"

"I certainly have." Walter Devan shook hands with a cordial grin. "I didn't know who I was picking a fight with at that time, though, or I'd have been a bit more careful about butting in."

"I'm glad you weren't," Simon said just as cordially, "or you might have done much too good a job."

"What do you think about the news from Russia?" Quennel asked.

So it was to be played like that. And the Saint was quite ready to go along with it that way. Perhaps he even preferred it. He had quite a little background to fill in, and in it he knew that there were things which were important to his philosophy, even if anyone else would have found them incidental. He could wait now for the explosive action which was ultimately the only way in which the difference of basic potential could be resolved, like the difference between two thunderclouds. But before that he was glad to explore and weigh the charge that was going to match itself against his own.

He lighted a cigarette, and relaxed, and for the first time since the beginning of the episode he knew that it had a significance beyond any simple violence that might come out of it.

They had another drink. And dinner. It was not a lavish dinner, but just quietly excellent, served by a butler whose presence didn't keep reminding you of the dignity of having a butler. There was not a dazzling display of silver and crystal on the table. They drank, without discussion or fanfares, an ex-

cellent Fountaingrove Sonoma Cabernet. Everything had the cachet of a man to whom luxury was
as natural and essential as a daily bath, without
making a De Mille sequence out of it.

"I think you'll like Pinehurst, if Andrea takes you
down there," Quennel said. "I just got a couple of
new strings of polo ponies from Buenos Aires—I
haven't even seen them yet. You might be able to
try them out for me. Do you play polo?"

"A bit," said the Saint, who had once had a six-
goal rating.

"I can't wait to get down there myself," said
Quennel. "But Washington never stops conspiring
against me."

"I imagine the war has something to do with it,
too."

Quennel nodded.

"It has made us pretty important," he said depre-
catingly. "We were doing quite all right before, but
war-time requirements are making us expand very
considerably. Of course, we're working about
ninety-five per cent on Government orders now.
But after the war we'll really have the advantage of
a tremendous amount of building and plant ex-
pansion, as well as some great strides in technical
experience."

"All of which the Government, meaning the people, will have given you and paid for," Simon observed sympathetically.

"Yes." Quennel accepted it quite directly and
disarmingly. "We don't expect to do any profiteering at this time, and in any case the tax system
wouldn't let us, but in the end we shall get our return—fundamentally in improved methods and increased capital values, which good management
will turn back into income."

Simon made idle mosaics with a fork in the things on his plate; and presently he said: "How have you been making out with labor problems in your field?"

"We really don't have any labor trouble. All our plants are in the South, of course, where you get less of that sort of thing than anywhere else. Labor is always a bit of a problem in these days, but I honestly think it only boils down to knowing how to handle your employees. How about it, Walter?— that's your headache."

"Quenco pays as good wages as any other industry in our areas," Devan said ruggedly. "And I think we do as much to look after them as any other firm you can mention. You'd be surprised at what we do. We have our own health insurance, and our own group clinics—we organise all kinds of social and athletic clubs for them—we even build their homes and finance them."

"That," said the Saint, "is the sort of thing that makes some of the things one hears so puzzling."

"What things?"

"I mean some of the rumors—you must have heard them yourself—about your private Gestapo, and that kind of talk."

Devan smiled with his strong confident mouth.

"Of course we have our private plant investigators. You couldn't possibly handle thousands of employees like we have without them. But when they aren't looking for cases of petty larceny and organised laziness, which you have to contend with in any outfit as big as ours, they're mostly just keeping in touch with the morale of the staff. That's the only way we can really insure against trouble, by anticipating it before it comes."

"That's one of the crosses we have to bear,"

Quennel said. "I'd like to know any other company that hasn't been smeared with the same gossip."

"I suppose so," Simon agreed flexibly. "But it must be specially tough when there's an accident they can hang it on. Like those union organisers who got killed in the riot at Mobile last year, for instance."

Devan made a blunt admissive movement of his head.

"Things like that are bound to happen sometimes. It was too bad it had to be us. But some of our people have been with us a long time, and you'd be surprised what a strong feeling they've got about the company. When some cheap racketeering rabble-rousers come around trying to stir up trouble, they can't help getting sore, and then somebody may get hurt."

"After all," Quennel said, "we aren't fighting a war against Fascism to make the country safe for the Communists. We're fighting for liberty and democracy, and that automatically means that we're also fighting to preserve the kind of social stability that liberty and democracy have built up in this country."

"What particular kind of social stability were you thinking of?" Simon asked.

"I mean a proper and progressive relationship between Capital and Labor. I don't believe in Labor run wild. No sensible man does. Without any revolutions, we've been slowly improving the conditions and standards of Labor, but we haven't disrupted our economic framework to do it. We believe that all men were created free and equal, but we admit that they don't all develop equal abilities. Therefore, for a long time to come, there are bound to be great masses of people who need to be restrained and controlled and brought along gradually. We don't need storm troopers and concentration camps to do it, because we have a sound economic system which obtains the same results in a much more civilised way. But we do have to recognise, and we do tacitly recognise, that we can't do without a strong and capable executive class who know how to nurse these masses along and feed them their rights in reasonable doses."

There was a weird fascination, a hypnotic rationality about the discussion, in those terms and at that moment, with everything that was tied up with it and looming over it, which had a certain dreamlike quality that was weirder and worse because it was not a dream. But the Saint would not have let it break up uncompleted even if he could.

He said, in exactly the same way as he had listened: "I wonder if it's only what you might call the lower classes who need nursing along."

"Who else are you thinking of?"

"I'm thinking of what the same terminology would call the upper classes. I suppose—the people that you and I both spend a lot of our time with. I wonder, for instance, if they've got just as clear an idea that there's a war on and what it's all about."

"I should say they've got just as clear an idea."

"I wish I were so sure," said the Saint, out of that same detachment. "I've looked at them. I've tried to get a feeling about them. They buy War Bonds. They submit to having their sugar rationed. They wonder how the hell they're going to keep up with their taxes. They grumble and connive a bit about tires and gasoline. They read the newspapers and become barroom strategists. Some of them have been put out of business—just as some of them have found new bonanzas. Some of them have been closer to the draft than others. But it still isn't real."

"I think it's very real."

"It isn't real. Thousands of men dying in some bloody Russian swamp are just newspaper figures. Prisoners being tortured and mutilated and bayoneted in the Far East are just good horror reading like a good thriller from the library. They haven't been hurt themselves. It's going to be all right. The war is expensive and inconvenient, but it's going to be all right. It's all going to be taken care of eventually. That's what we pay taxes for."

"Everybody can't do the fighting," said Devan. "In these days it takes—I forget the exact statistics, but I read them somewhere—something like ten people working at home to keep one soldier at the front."

"But the people behind the lines have to feel just as sure as the soldier that they're in a war. They've got to feel that the whole course and purpose of their lives has been changed, just as his has—and you don't feel that just from getting by on one pound of sugar a week. They've got to have something that the people of England have got, because their war was never thousands of miles away. It's something that you only get from going hungry, and walking in the dark at night, and seeing things you've grown up with destroyed, and watching your friends die. That's when you know you're really in a war, whatever job you happen to be doing, and literally fighting for your life, and everything has to go into it. There isn't that feeling here yet. I think there are still too many people who sincerely think that all they have to do is root for the home team. I think there are still too many people who think you can fight total war on a basis of golf as usual every Saturday and nothing must be allowed to interfere with our dear old social stability. Particularly the people who ought to be leading in the opposite direction. Particularly," said the Saint carefully, "the wrong people."

Quennel made a slight impatient gesture.

"I can't think where you'd get that impression. Where have you been lately?"

"I was in Florida for a while. And then I was in New York for a couple of weeks."

"And in New York I suppose you go to El Morocco and 21 and places like that."

"I don't live there, but I've been to them. They seem to be doing all right."

Quennel raised his shoulders triumphantly.

"Then of course you'd get a wrong impression. The class of people you find in those places—in Miami Beach and Palm Beach and New York night clubs—they're a class that this war is going to wipe out completely. They're dead now, but they don't know it."

He settled back confidently, efficiently, and took a cigar from the box which the unobtrusive butler was passing. He lighted it and tasted it approvingly, and said: "I'm glad I remembered to keep some of these locked up."

"Mice, or pixies?" Simon inquired with a smile.

"Just Andrea's friends," Quennel said tolerantly. "She throws parties for them up here all the time, and they go through the place like locusts. She had one only a week ago, and they drank up thirty cases of champagne, and that wasn't enough. They got into the cellar and finished half a dozen bottles of Benedictine that I was saving."

It came upon the Saint like the deep tolling of a bell in the far distance, like the resonance of an alarm that he had known about and been waiting

for, and yet which had to be actually heard before
it could compress the diaphragm and be felt throb-
bing out along the veins. But he knew now that this
was it, and that it was the last of everything that
had been missing, and that now he had seen all of
his dragon, and he knew all the ugliness and the evil
of it, and it was a bigger and sleeker dragon than he
had ever seen before.

He bent his head for a moment so that it should
not show in his face before he was quite ready,
while it went through him like light would have
gone through his eyes, and while he tapped and
lighted a cigarette because he didn't feel like a
cigar; and Hobart Quennel must have felt that
there was an implied submission in his withdrawal,
because Simon could feel it in the way Quennel settled himself back in his chair and told the butler to
bring in some brandy, the solid good humor of a
man who has made a rightful point. But when Simon looked up he looked at Andrea, who had been
silent for a long while, only following the argument
with her eyes from face to face. She was the one
person who until then had been physically in the
picture more than either of the two men, and yet
she had never been a fixed part of the composition.
He wondered whether she ever would have any
such place, or whether it was only an insatiable ar-
tistic sense of his own that made him imagine that
she should have found one.

He said lightly: "You must know a lot of gay people."

"I like parties," she said. She added, almost defiantly: "I like El Morocco, too, when I'm in the
mood. I don't see how it's going to help us win the
war if everybody sits around being miserable."

But she went on looking at the Saint, and her

eyes were still like windows opening on to an empty sky. You could look through them and out and out and there was still nothing but the clear pale blue and nothing.

Quennel smiled indulgently, and said: "It's pretty cool tonight. Why don't you go and get a fire started in the library, and we'll join you in a few minutes."

She got up.

"Don't forget you had something you wanted to tell Simon," she said.

"No—I was just thinking of that."

She had to look at the Saint again before she went out.

"Daddy always wants to have his own way," she said rather vaguely. "Don't let him keep you here for ever."

"I won't," said the Saint, with a last upward glance. Then the door closed behind her, and he was alone with one last sudden disturbing question in his mind, but quite alone, like a fighter when the gong sounds and the seconds disappear through the ropes. He knew that this was the gong, and the preliminary routines were over; and he knew just what he was fighting, and all his senses were keyed and calm and ice-cold. He turned to Quennel just as easily as he had played every waiting line of the scene, and murmured: "Andrea did say you had something to tell me."

Quennel trimmed his cigar on the ashtray in front of him.

"Yes," he said. "Andrea told me you were taking an interest in Calvin Gray's synthetic rubber, so I thought you'd like to know. Gray showed me a sample of it not long ago, as I think Walter told you. I had a report on it from my chief chemist today." He settled even more safely and positively in his chair. "I'm afraid Calvin Gray is a complete fraud."

2

Simon's right hand rested on the table in front of him like a bronze casting set on stone, and he watched the smoke rising from his cigarette like a pastel stroke against the dark wood.

"You had a specimen analysed?"

"Yes. I don't know whether you know it, but that kind of analysis is one of the most difficult things in the world to do. In fact, a lot of people would say it was almost impossible. But I've got some rather unusual men on my staff."

"Did you ever see it made?" Simon asked slowly.

"No."

"I have."

"Can you describe the process?"

Simon gave a rough description of what he had seen. He knew that it was technically meaningless, and admitted it.

"That doesn't matter," said Quennel. "I'm sure you can see now where the trick was worked."

"You mean in the enclosed electrical gadget, I suppose."

"Naturally," Quennel chuckled. "I'm surprised that a fellow like you wouldn't have caught on to it at once. It's just a dressed-up topical version of all those old swindles where a man has a machine that prints dollar bills or a formula for making diamonds."

"But why should a man like Calvin Gray go in for anything like that?"

"Do you know Calvin Gray?"

"Not personally. But I've checked on him, and

his reputation is quite special."

"But as I understand it, you haven't even seen him. All you've met is a pretty girl with a story."

"I've been to his house."

"How do you know it was his house? Because the girl took you there and told you it was?"

"*Who's Who* gives his residence as Stamford, Connecticut."

"I suppose that would be the only residence there."

The Saint's blue gaze was meditative and unimpassioned. He drew at his cigarette and set his wrist back on the table.

"Mind you," said Quennel, "I'm not necessarily suggesting that that's the answer. It could have been Gray's house. It could have been his daughter. It isn't impossible. It takes a big man to put over a big fraud."

"But why should Gray bother? I understood he was well enough off already."

"Who did you get that from? From the same source—from his daughter, or from the girl who said she was his daughter?"

"Yes," said the Saint thoughtfully.

Quennel trimmed his cigar again.

"Suppose it's what you were told from a good source. In business, that isn't always enough. A lot of men have had big reputations, and have been generally believed to be pretty well off, and have been well off—and still they've ended up in jail. I'm sure you can remember plenty of them yourself. Famous stockbrokers, attorneys, promoters . . . Not that I'm committing myself about this case. I don't know enough about it. Maybe Calvin Gray would be the most surprised man in the world if he knew about it. He might be away somewhere—lecturing, for instance—and his house might have been broken into and used by some gang of crooks. Even that's been done before. I don't have to tell you about these things. The only thing I think you ought to know is that this synthetic rubber story is a fraud."

Simon Templar took one more measured breath at his cigarette, and said: "I don't know how much you claim to know, but you may have heard that in Washington night before last there was an attempt to kidnap Madeline Gray, or the girl who calls herself Madeline Gray. Mr. Devan was there."

Devan nodded.

"That's right. Only I didn't know it was a kidnaping attempt, until Andrea gave us the idea after she'd talked to you."

"If it ever was a kidnaping attempt," said Quennel. "Or couldn't it have been part of the same build-up, staged for your benefit, to help make the case look important to you?"

The Saint had an odd ludicrous feeling of being a feed man, of offering properly baited hooks to fish who had personally chosen the bait. But he had to hear all the answers; he had to see the whole scene played through.

"You wouldn't have heard it," he said, "but it seems as if Calvin Gray really was kidnaped."

"Really?"

"At any rate, either he or the man who is being talked about is missing." Simon paused casually. "I've already called in the FBI about it."

There was silence for a moment. It had a curious negative quality, as if it were more than a mere incidental absence of sound and movement, as if it would have absorbed and neutralised any sound or movement there had been.

"What about the girl?" Devan asked; and Simon met his crinkly deep-set eyes.

"Since this afternoon," he said expressionlessly, "she seems to be missing too."

There was only a barely perceptible flicker of stillness this time, as if a movie projector had stuck on the same frame for two or three extra spins of the shutter. And then Hobart Quennel moved a little, and drank some brandy, and raised one shoulder to settle his forearm more comfortably on the arm of his chair.

"Probably it was your calling in the FBI that did that," he said. "That would have been a complication they weren't expecting."

"Why?"

"You always had a reputation—forgive me, I'm not being personal, but after all we all read newspapers—for being a sort of lone wolf. So the last thing they'd have expected was that you'd take your troubles to any of the authorities. In fact, I'm a little surprised about it myself."

"These aren't quite the same times," said the Saint quietly. "And perhaps a few things have changed for me as they have for everyone else."

Quennel laughed a little, his sound sure confident laugh.

"Anyway," he said, "probably you scared them, and now they're organising a nice neat getaway. You can take it that the whole deal was crooked from the beginning anyhow, whatever the minor details were . . . Very possibly the real Calvin Gray will turn up in a day or two, and be as puzzled as anyone . . . It doesn't really make a lot of difference, does it?"

"It makes a difference," said the Saint; and his voice was as even as a calm arctic bay, and the same invisible chill nestled over it. He said: "I go after crooks."

Hobart Quennel's slight deep engaging chuckle came again like a breath from the South, and now it was warmer and surer than ever, and there was no uncertainty at all left behind in it, and it could soothe you and blot the search and the questioning and the fight out of you like the breeze rustling through southern palms; and it was right, it had to be right, because nothing could be wrong that was so friendly and permanent and sure.

"I know," he said. "But you just said it yourself. These aren't the same times, and everybody changes. This Gray business will take care of itself now. If you've already called in the FBI, it's sure to. It's in good hands. It's none of my business, but I can't really see you wasting any more time on it. It wouldn't do you justice."

"What would?" Simon asked.

Quennel turned his cigar again.

"Well, frankly, I've read a lot about you and I've often thought that you weren't doing yourself justice, even before the war. Not that I haven't enjoyed your exploits. But it's always seemed to me that a man with your mind and your abilities could have achieved so much more . . . You know, sometimes I've wondered whether a man like you mayn't have been suffering from some mistaken ideas about business. I don't mean selling things over the counter in a hardware store. I mean the kind of business that I do."

"Perhaps I don't know enough about it."

"I assure you it can be just as great an adventure, in its own way, as anything you've ever done. A great corporation is like a little empire. Its relations with other corporations and industries are like the relations between empires. You have diplomacy, alliances, feuds, espionage, and wars. Quite often you have to step right through ordinary laws and restrictions. That's one of the things I meant by the necessity for a strong executive class. I think if you go into it you'll find that they are really only paralleling your own attitude. There have to be a great many petty general regulations for the conduct of the majority of people, just as there have to be for children. It's just as necessary for there to be parents, and people who can step above the ordinary regulations. I think you'd find yourself quite at home in that class. I think that business could employ all your brilliance, all your charm, all your audacity, all your generalship, all your—shall I say —ruthlessness."

"You could be right," said the Saint, with a smile that barely touched the edges of his mouth. "But who would give me a job?"

"I would," said Quennel.

The Saint gazed at him.

"You would?"

"Yes," Quennel said deliberately. "To be quite truthful, when I told Andrea to ask you over, I was thinking about that much more than about the Gray business. Let's say it was one of my crazy ideas, or one of my hunches. You don't get very far in business without having those ideas. I believe right now a man like you could be worth a hundred thousand dollars a year to me."

Simon drew his glass closer to him and cupped it in his hand, the stem between his second and third fingers, making gentle movements that swirled the golden spirit softly around and warmed it in the curve of the bowl.

This, then, was all of it, and all the answers and

explanations were there. And he knew quite certainly now, as his intuition had always told him, that there was no ordinary way to fight it. As Quennel had said, there were times when you had to step right through ordinary laws and restrictions. There was a world outside the orderly lawful world of average people, and to fight anyone there you had to move completely into his world, or else he was as untouchable and invulnerable as if he were in another dimension.

The Saint smiled a little, very sardonically and deep inside himself, at the passing thought of how far he would have been likely to get if he had tried to fight Hobart Quennel from any footing on the commonplace world. Even without his own peculiar reputation by commonplace legal standards, he knew how ridiculous the accusations he would have had to make would have seemed when thrown against such a man as Quennel. It wouldn't be merely because of Quennel's wealth. It would be because his standing, his respect, his utterly genuine confidence and authority and rightness and integrity would throw off anything the Saint could say like armor would throw off spitballs.

It was a good thing, Simon thought, that he also could move in dimensions where such considerations were only words.

He finished his brandy, enjoying the full savor of the last sip, and put the glass down, and said pleasantly: "That's very flattering. But I have another idea."

"What is that?"

Unhurriedly, almost idly, the Saint put his right hand under his coat, under his left arm, and brought out the automatic that rode there. He leveled it diagonally across the table, letting the aim of its dark blunt sleek muzzle touch Quennel and Devan in turn.

"This is what I was talking about before," he said. "About the war being close to home. The war is here with you now, Quennel. I came here for Calvin Gray and his daughter, and unless I get them I promise you some of us are going to die most unexpectedly."

The only trouble was, as the Saint reckoned it afterwards, that even then he still hadn't realized deeply enough how closely Quennel's—or at least Devan's—fourth-dimensional mentality might coincide with his own.

He looked at their rigid immobility, at Quennel's face still bland and bony and Walter Devan's face heavy and grim, both of them staring at him soberly and calculatingly but without any abrupt panic; and then he saw Devan's eyes flick fractionally upwards to a point in space just above his head.

Instantly, and before Simon could move at all, a new voice spoke behind him. It was a voice with a rich bass croak that Simon seemed to have heard before, very recently.

"Okay," said the voice. "Hold it. Don't move anything if you want to go out of here breathing."

The Saint held it. He knew quite well where he had heard that deep grating voice before.

It spoke again, sounding a little nearer.

"I been saving this for you, bud," it said.

After that there was only a fierce jarring agony that crashed through the Saint's skull like a bolt of lightning, with a scorching white light that broke into a million rainbow stars that danced away into a deep engulfing darkness.

3

Coming back to consciousness was a distant brilliance that hurt his eyes even through his closed eyelids, a sharp cold wet monotonous nagging slapping on his cheeks that turned out to be a sodden towel unsympathetically wielded by Karl Morgen.

"That's enough, Karl," said Walter Devan's voice.

Simon rubbed his face with his hands and cleared his eyes. The tall raw-boned man stood over him, looking as if he would enjoy repeating both the assault and the remedy.

"Beat it, Karl," Devan said.

Morgen went out reluctantly.

Simon tried to get his bearings in a rather unusual room. It was small and somewhat bare. The walls and ceiling were plain white cement, and they looked new and clean. There was a plain new-looking carpet on the floor. There was the plain heavy unpainted door through which Karl had gone out, and another identical door in another wall. Near the ceiling in one wall was a sort of open embrasure, but it was too high up to see out of from where the Saint sat. There was no other window.

The Saint sat on a simple divan with blankets over it, and on the opposite side of the room was another similar divan. There were some low shelves against another wall on which he saw a small radiophone, some records, half a dozen books, a couple of packs of cards, a bottle of brandy, a bottle of Scotch, a box of chocolates, half a dozen cans of assorted food, and a package of paper plates. The air had a slightly damp chill in it.

"People in stories always ask 'Where am I?' " said the Saint, "so I will."

"This is Mr. Quennel's private air-raid shelter," replied Devan. "He had it built about a year ago."

He sat in a comfortable chair behind a card table, smoking a freshly lighted cigar. He wielded the cigar with his left hand, because his right hand held an automatic which the Saint recognised as his own. He didn't point the gun. His hand was relaxed with it on the table. But he was twelve feet from the Saint, and pointing was not necessary.

"Very nice it looks," Simon murmured. "And handy," he added.

"Cigarette?" Devan tossed a pack into the Saint's lap, and followed it with a book of matches. "Keep 'em," he said. "I'm afraid Karl took everything you had away from you."

"Naturally."

Simon didn't have to check over his pockets and other hiding places. He had no doubt that the search would have been thorough. An intellectual organization like that wouldn't have risked leaving anything that could conceivably have concealed some ingenious means of making unexpected trouble.

He lighted a cigarette and said reminiscently: "Karl really owes you something, after Washington. You did a nice job of looking after him and his pal."

Devan nodded.

"It was the only thing to do."

"You took quite a risk."

"I couldn't expect people to take risks for me if they didn't know I'd do the same for them. I took a bit of a beating, too, if you haven't forgotten. That's why I'm keeping this gun handy, and I want you to stay sitting down where you are."

Simon grinned wryly.

"Have you been saving something for me too?"

Devan shook his head.

"Let's forget that. That's kid stuff. I'm here because Bart asked me to see if I couldn't talk you into reconsidering his proposition, and that's all I want to do."

"You've been studying all the best Nazi heavies in the movies," said the Saint admiringly. "I see all the delicate touches. And when I go on saying No, you most regretfully call back the storm troopers and they beat the bejesus out of me."

"I'm not a Nazi, Templar. Neither is Mr. Quennel."

"You have some unusual thugs on your staff. I'll bet you Karl heils Hitler every time he goes to the bathroom."

"I'm not concerned about that. When Gray fired him and he came to us, I thought he could be useful. He has been. So long as he does what I tell him I don't have to ask about his politics. He isn't going to find out any Quenco secrets. And I know one thing—being what he is, no matter what happens, he can't squawk."

"Now I really know what Quennel meant about the diplomacy of Big Business," said the Saint. "Getting a German spy to do your dirty work for you ought to be worth some kind of Oscar."

"We've been lucky to have the use of him. But that's the only connection there is. I'm an American, and I don't want to be anything else."

"I know all about you, Walter. I could tell you your own life story. I've read a very complete secret dossier on you. Oh, I know there's nothing in it that could put you in jail, or you'd have been there before this. But the indication is quite definite. You are Quennel's chief private thug, which means his own personal Gestapo."

Devan sat still, with only a slight dull red glow under his skin.

"There's nothing Nazi about it. If you know all about us, you know that we're working one hundred per cent for America. I work for Quennel because he has to have a man who can be tough and handle tough situations. He told you himself—an industry like Quenco is like a little empire. You have to have your own police and your own laws and your own enforcement. This is nothing but business."

"Business, because Calvin Gray's invention would shift a great big slice of Government backing away from you, and you'd be in the hole to the extent of your own investment."

"As Mr. Quennel said, it's not going to be any use winning the war if we win it by ruining our own economic structure."

"How catching his phrases are," drawled the Saint. "I suppose it wouldn't have occurred to you that Mr. Quennel might have been thinking first of Mr. Quennel's own economic structure?"

"We aren't Nazis," Devan reiterated stubbornly.

Simon drew a fresh drift of smoke into his lungs.

"No," he said. "You aren't Nazis. Or even conscious fifth columnists. That's one of the things that bothered me for a while. I couldn't understand the half-hearted villainy. The Nazis would have been much more positive and drastic, and Calvin Gray and his invention would probably have been mopped up long ago."

"We don't like violence," Devan said. "It makes trouble and a stink and it's dangerous, and we bend over backwards to avoid it. Only sometimes it's forced on us, and then we have to be able to handle it. We tried to handle Gray without going too far."

"And the hell with what difference it made to the net cost and efficiency of our war production?"

"Superficial savings and efficiencies aren't always the best when you take a broad long view. You learn that in a big industry. Mr. Quennel knows all about that, because that's his job."

"The Führer principle," Simon observed, almost to himself. He looked at Devan again, and said: "And now that I've really butted in, and you know you're stuck with it?"

"The sky's the limit."

Simon smoked again, and looked at the end of his cigarette. "You think you can get away with it?"

"I'm sure we can."

"There's a little matter of murder involved, and the police take such an oldfashioned view of that."

"You're talking about Angert? That was stupid of Morgen, but he didn't mean to kill him. He didn't know who he was. But that'll be Morgen's bad luck, if he gets caught. I'll try to see that he doesn't get caught. But if he did, we wouldn't know anything about him."

"You ought to worry about being caught yourself. If you read the papers, you may have seen something about a certain Inspector Fernack, who has just gotten ambitious about collecting the scalp of the guy who removed a very dull bureaucrat named Imberline last night—and nearly managed to hang the job on me."

Devan looked him straight in the eye.

"I read the papers. But I wasn't anywhere near the Savoy Plaza last night. And I thought Imberline was still in Washington."

That was his story. And probably he could prove it. Quennel could probably prove the same. It

would be very careless of them if they couldn't, and
the Saint didn't think they were careless. If they
had been addicted to making egregious mistakes,
someone else would have taken care of them before
he ever came along.

It was a rather depressing thought. But he had to
finish covering the ground. He took another breath
through his cigarette.

"A man like Calvin Gray, and his daughter, can't
just disappear without any questions being asked."

"Calvin Gray won't disappear. He'll be back
tomorrow from a visit to some friends in Tennessee,
and he'll be very surprised at the commotion. His
daughter will have gone to New York with some
friends—who have an apartment there, by the way
—and he will have reached her on the telephone
there. When she hears that it's all a false alarm and
he's quite all right, she will tell him that she's going
on a trip to Cuba with some other friends. From
there she'll probably fly down to Rio. She may even
get married down there and not come back for a
very long time."

The Saint's eyes were cold and realistic.

"And of course Gray will go along with that."

"I think so, after I've had another talk with him.
I think he'll even discover that there was a flaw in
his formula after all, and forget about it."

"You aren't even interested in it yourselves?"

"Oh, yes of course he'll have to tell us the formula. It may be valuable one day, if we have one of
our own chemists discover it. But for the present
Mr. Quennel is quite satisfied with our own setup."

"And Gray will never open his mouth so long as
you have his daughter for a hostage."

Devan shrugged.

"I don't have to be melodramatic with you. You know what these things are all about. You know what he'll do."

The Saint knew. There was heroism of a kind for the lone individual, although even that could almost always be broken down eventually under pitiless scientific treatment. He doubted how much ultimate heroism there would ever be against the peril of a man's own daughter.

He didn't doubt that Walter Devan was the man to see the job through competently and remorselessly. Devan was no common thug, or he would not have had the position he held. He could easily have passed as having had a college education, even if most of it had been spent on the football field. He had a definite intelligence. He really belonged in Quennel's entourage. He had enough intelligence to assimilate Quennel's intellectual arguments. He also believed in what he was doing, and he was just as sure that it was right. And he wouldn't make any stupid mistakes. Simon didn't need to press him for elaborate details. Walter Devan would know just how to finish what he had started.

There was only one question left in the Saint's mind.

"How does Andrea feel about all this?" he asked.

"Andrea doesn't think," Devan said casually. "She does a sort of roping job for Bart now and again. He probably told her you might be connected with someone who was trying to put over a dirty deal on him in business. He wouldn't tell her anything else. But she seems to be carrying quite a torch for you." Devan met the Saint's gaze with brash man-to-man candor. "You're on your own, as far as that goes. She could be a lot of fun."

"If I played ball," said the Saint.

Devan made an affirmative movement with his head and his cigar at the same time.

"Why be a dope? You can't win. But there aren't any hard feelings. Bart and I both appreciate what you've done, and what you're after. And the proposition he made you still goes. One hundred per cent."

"But if I turn you down—"

"Why bring that up? I don't have to tell you we can't leave you around now. But you belong with us."

Simon glanced at the stump of his cigarette. Having been warned once, he didn't try to get up and move towards the ashtray that Devan was using. He trod the cigarette out on the carpet, and lighted another.

He had heard the threat of death many times in his life, but never with such utter certainty and conviction. Even though not a word had been said about it at all. It gave him a sense of frozen inevitability that no noise and savagery could have done. And he knew that Walter Devan was just as aware of it as he was. They spoke the same language so closely that it would have been merely a waste of energy to shout . . .

Devan stood up, still holding the gun.

"Why don't you take a few minutes to think it over?" he said.

He went to the door through which the long bigboned man had gone out; and as he opened it he jerked his head towards the second door.

"Calvin Gray and his daughter are in the next room," he said. "Say hullo to them if you want to."

Simon Templar was alone.

He got to his feet after a moment, surveyed the room once more in a detached way, and turned to the other door.

It opened when he tried the handle, and he went in.

It was a room very much like the one he had left. Madeline Gray and her father sat side by side on a divan close to the door. It had to be Calvin Gray, of course, before she jumped up and introduced them.

"How do you do," said the Saint.

They shook hands. A strange formality, and a stranger tribute to the perdurance of common customs.

Madeline Gray left her hand resting on the Saint's arm, and he smiled down at her and said: "How soundproof are the doors?"

"We heard all of it, in the other room," she said.

It was all very quiet; and when you came down to it there didn't seem to be any other way it could be.

"Then we can save a lot of repetition," said the Saint. "I don't even care very much about the details of how you two were snatched. It's relatively unimportant now."

"What were you saying in there," she asked, "about Imberline?"

"They killed him."

He told them all about that, from the dossiers he had studied through to his session with Fernack in the morning. He skipped as lightly as he could through the interval he had spent with Andrea. He gave her credit for having tried to keep him out of that trap without telling him about it, but he didn't elaborate on the counter-attractions she had offered. But he saw Madeline watching him rather thoughtfully.

"In one way," he said grimly, "you could say that

I killed him. Just like I got the two of you into this. By being, too clever . . . You were quite wrong about him. On the evidence, he had to be honest. So I went to him as an honest man—to see if I couldn't convert him to our side. I wasn't able to do that in five minutes—it took him too long to understand anything that wasn't a proverb—but at least I figured that I'd laid up some more trouble for the Ungodly. Unfortunately, I had. But I didn't know he'd be seeing Quennel and Devan that same night. And even after I saw Devan downstairs, I didn't think of it in the right way. I suppose they were having this conference in New York because too many people are watching too many other people's maneuvers in Washington; they knew by then that the ice was awful thin and getting thinner by the minute with me breathing on it, and they had to make sure they could keep Imberline where they wanted him. Instead of that, they got just the reverse. Suspicion had started to penetrate into that mess of porridge he used for a brain, and there was no talking him out of it. When he checked with Jetterick, they knew they were up against it. They may have tried threats or bribery at that point, but he was just too stubborn or stupid to be scared or bought—it doesn't make any difference now. There was only one way to stop him then; and they stopped him."

"But we still want to know how you got here," said the girl huskily.

Simon's glance reflexed to the doors again. But it didn't really matter. He had nothing to say just then that couldn't be overheard.

"I'll tell you," he said.

He lay on the other divan and told them, stretched out in an amazing restful relaxation that was not actually any testimonial to the steel in his nerves at all, but only to the supreme conservation of energy that a trapped tiger would have had.

He told them everything he had thought from the beginning; and in as much detail as he could remember he gave them an account of the dinner conversation in which so many things had been so elementarily explained.

He tried to do a good job of it; but he still didn't know how well he had made his point when he had finished reporting and Calvin Gray said: "How can a man like Quennel be like that?"

He was a fairly tall wiry man, lean almost to the verge of emaciation, with a tousled mop of perfectly white hair and eyes that blinked with nervous frequency behind square rimless glasses; and he said it with an air of academic perplexity, as if he were fretting over a chemical paradox.

The Saint put one hand behind his head and gazed at the ceiling.

"Simply because he is a man like that. Because he's more dangerous than any fifth columnist or any outright crook, because he sincerely believes that he's a just and important and progressive citizen. Because he can talk contemptuously about Café Society and the playboy class, and really believe it and feel austerely superior to them, and sandwich it in between mentioning his new strings of polo ponies and the parties he throws for his daughter where they drink thirty cases of champagne. 'They're dead but they don't know it'—but he's one of them and he doesn't know it . . . Because he can disclaim profiteering while he feels very contented about 'increased capital values' . . . Because he's very proud of his share in the War Effort, but he thinks nothing of faking the registration of the family cars so as to get more than his share of gas to play with. Because he doesn't mind using a German agent like Morgen if Morgen can be useful, instead of turning him over to the FBI; but he'd be full of righteous indignation if you called him a fifth columnist . . . Because he hates Fascism and he's a patriotic one-hundred-per-cent American; but he believes in what he calls 'social stability' and 'a strong and capable executive class' whose divine mission it is to dish out liberty and democracy in reasonable doses to the dumb unruly proletariat . . . Because he's thoroughly satisfied that Big Business is wide awake and wading into the war effort with both hands, but he's also ready to sabotage a rival process that would speed up and cheapen a very vital production, because it would lose him a hell of a lot of dough . . . Because he builds model homes and organizes baseball teams and sewing bees for his employees to keep them happy, but he believes that nabobs like himself should have a law of their own which transcends the rights of ordinary mortals . . . Because he's exactly the same type as Thyssen and the other Big Business men who backed Hitler to preserve their own kind of Social Stability; because he'd back his own kind of dictatorship in this country, under another name, and still think what a fine level-headed liberal he was . . . Because he's a goddam bloody Nazi himself, and you can never hang it on him because even he hasn't begun to realise it."

His voice seemed to linger in the air, so quiet and sensible, and yet with a feeling so much deeper than any dramatics, so that it seemed as if it should have gone on for ever, and there should have been some thing permanent about it, and it should have spread out whenever the minds of those who listened would take it on.

Calvin Gray rubbed his rough white hair and said hazily: "But when he goes into actual crime—"

"Quennel," said the Saint, "never went into a crime in his life. If he tells Devan that you and your invention are a Bad Thing, and ought to be stopped, he's only giving his opinion. If things happen to you and stop you, he's naturally very pleased about it. If he tells Devan to try and talk me into forgetting you and taking a job with Quenco, that's entirely legitimate. If Devan succeeds, fine. If he doesn't, but an unfortunate accident eliminates me, that's providential . . . It would have been the same with Imberline. I don't doubt that Quennel finally went off and left Devan to go on arguing. If Devan could talk Imberline around, that would be swell. If Imberline dropped dead in the bathroom before the argument was settled, that was too bad, but it saved a whole lot of trouble."

"But he tried to tell you I was a fraud."

"A diplomatic fiction. And very well done. If it hadn't been me, he might easily have put it over. And even if it didn't completely go over, it might still have served—with the offer of a wonderful job to wash it down. I could have helped myself to believe it, if I'd wanted to: it would have been a fair enough excuse to stop worrying about you and put my conscience to sleep. But it was no crime."

Calvin Gray shook his head helplessly.

"The man must be insane. It's such incredible hypocrisy."

"It's not hypocrisy. And he's perfectly sane. He just doesn't ask what methods Devan uses, and therefore he doesn't know. He could probably justify them out of his philosophy if he had to, but his great mind is occupied with so many more important things that it's much simpler not to know. I don't suppose Hitler ever does any positive thinking about what happens to prisoners in Dachau, either."

There was silence for a little while, an odd calm silence that made it almost fantastic to think that this was a profoundly philosophical conversation in a bright and comfortable death cell.

It was the girl who brought it back to that.

"You don't think Devan is bluffing at all?" she said.

"Not for an instant," said the Saint gently, "Don't let's waste any effort kidding ourselves about that. Devan will arrange whatever he has to arrange, and he'll do as neat a job as I could do myself."

Her brown eyes that smiled so easily were big and deep and unflinching.

"Don't worry about it," he answered carelessly. "If it hadn't been this, it would have been something else."

She looked around the room.

"Isn't there any way you could get out?"

He laughed a little, and got back on his feet.

"If there were, I wouldn't be here. I tell you, our Walter isn't an amateur."

But he strolled over to the high embrasure like the one he had noticed in the other room. Standing on a chair, he saw that it sloped downwards towards the outside, and at the outside was a heavy steel venetian shutter. He guessed that the shelter was built in the side of the hill running down to the Sound, and the embrasure peeped out through the hillside, providing natural ventilation but still safe from the blast of anything but a direct hit on the opening. The steel shutter was set solidly in the concrete, and he took one look at it and stepped down with a shrug.

"Why can't you tell Quennel that you'll accept his offer?" asked Gray. "Then, later on, you'd have a chance—"

"Do you imagine they haven't thought of that?" Simon retorted patiently. "I think Quennel meant every word of his offer, and I think he still means it in spite of everything, and I'm sure he'd live up to it to the letter; but I'm also sure that he'd want to be damn certain that I was the same. I don't know what proof or security he'd want—I can think of half a dozen devices—but it doesn't matter. You can take it that it would be good."

He stood over Calvin Gray, poised and quiet and kindly implacable.

"This is your problem, not mine," he said.

The girl sat beside her father again and held his hand.

"You mustn't think about me," she said. "You mustn't."

"How can I help it?"

"If you were both tortured to death," said the Saint inexorably, "what good would it do?"

Calvin Gray covered his eyes.

"Devan talked to me all afternoon," he said hoarsely. "He told me . . . If it was only myself, I could try . . . But Madeline. I'm not big enough . . . And what good would it do? What difference would it make? They'll kill the invention anyway. So why should . . ." His voice broke, and then rose suddenly. "I couldn't see it. Don't you understand? I couldn't!"

"Daddy," said the girl.

The Saint watched for an instant, and then turned away.

On one of the side shelves, beside the playing cards, there was a score pad and a pencil. He picked them up. At the top of the first sheet he printed in bold capitals: WE MAY BE OVERHEARD. Then under that he wrote a few quick lines. He tore off the sheet and put the pad and pencil back.

Then he returned to Calvin Gray and put a hand on his shoulder, and the old man looked up at him hollow-eyed.

"Crying won't get you anywhere. This is still a war," said the Saint, and handed him the paper he had written on.

The girl tried to lean over and see; but Simon took her arm and brought her up to her feet and led her a few steps away. He held her by both elbows, facing him, and gazed at her with all the strength that was in him.

"Some of this is my fault too," he said. "If I hadn't butted in, it might not have been so bad."

Then the door opened, and Walter Devan came in.

He looked like a sales manager who had left a conference room at a crucial moment to answer a phone call.

"Well?" he inquired briskly.

The Saint detached himself leisuredly, and lighted another cigarette.

"So far as I'm concerned," he said, without a flicker of emotion, "the answer is still: Nuts."

"So is mine," said the girl clearly.

"I'm sorry," said Devan; and it sounded like genuine regret.

But he looked at Calvin Gray.

Gray got up off the divan. He was unsteady and

haggard, and his eyes burned.

"Mine isn't," he said. "Can you swear to me that if I do everything you want, nothing will ever happen to Madeline?"

"Daddy!" said the girl.

"I can," said Devan.

The old man's hands twisted together.

"Then—I will."

Devan studied him, not with cheap triumph, but with sturdy businesslike satisfaction.

"I'll get you some paper to write out your process," he said, in quite a friendly way. "Is there anything else you'd like?"

Gray shook his head.

"I couldn't write it. It would sound so complicated, and—I don't even know if I could concentrate enough . . . Please . . . Can't you make it easy? Mr. Quennel used to be a chemist himself, didn't he? Take me back to my laboratory, I'll show him—"

"Daddy," said the girl in torment.

"I'll show him," Gray said in a kind of hysterical breathlessness. "He'll understand. And he'll have it all to himself. Nothing in writing. Him and me . . . and nobody'll ever know . . . and Madeline . . . You promise?"

"Come back to the house and talk to Mr. Quennel yourself," Devan said reasonably.

He took Calvin Gray's arm and steered him towards the door. But he never turned his back on the Saint; and, almost paralytically, his right hand stayed with the bulge in his coat pocket where it had been from the time when he came in.

Madeline Gray tensed in a spasmic impulse to go after him; and the Saint caught her by the shoulders and held her.

The door closed again.

Simon Templar's face was like stone.

"You can't do anything," he said.

It was a moment of interminable stillness.

Then with a fierce irresistible movement, she tore herself away from him and flung herself down on the nearest divan, face downwards, her face clutched and buried between her hands. He could see her right hand, the small fingers clenched to whiteness as the knuckles gripped at her temples.

After a while he lighted another cigarette and took to strolling slowly and silently up and down the room.

It must have been about ten minutes before she turned over on her back and lay with one fist at her mouth, staring blankly up at the ceiling. And only then he thought it might be safe to speak. And even then, he stood over her and kept his voice so low that it was only just enough to brush her ears.

He said softly: "Madeline."

"He didn't have to do it," she said tonelessly. "He didn't."

He said: "Madeline, this is very probably curtains for all of us, but we don't have to go alone. I gave him a note."

"It didn't make any difference."

"I hope it did. I believe it did. I told him what to do."

She sat up with a sudden start.

"You told him—what?"

"I told him we could still do something on our way. I told him to get Quennel over to the laboratory. And then I said I was sure that while he was pretending to demonstrate his process he could put some things together that would go off all at once with a loud noise. And it wouldn't do any of us any good, but it would take Quennel along too, and probably Devan with him. And in the end that may be just as important." The Saint's voice was very light, no more than a breath between iron lips that scarcely moved. "I sent him to die, Madeline, but in the best way that any of us could do it."

She was on her feet somehow. She was holding his arms by the sleeves, making little aimless tugging movements, rocking a little in a kind of anguish of inarticulacy. Her eyes were flooding and yet her lips were parted in an unearthly sort of smile.

"You did that?" she repeated again and again; and it was as if something sang through the break in her voice. "You did that?"

He nodded.

Then the door opened, and he turned sharply.

Andrea Quennel came in.

4

She said: "Hullo."

He looked into her pale empty eyes that still gave him nothing back, and put one hand negligently in his pocket, and said affably: "Hullo to you."

"What are you doing?"

"Rehearsing a play," he said.

"Why are you locked in here?"

He still didn't know how to take her.

"We heard that Selznick was looking for us," he said, "so we were going to be very inaccessible and make him double his offer."

"I thought there was something wrong," she said. "I've seen silly things happen to people who crossed Daddy before. I don't usually worry, because I'm not superstitious, but I was worried about you. So I watched. I saw them carry you out here. And that was even after I tried to warn you to be careful when I left the dining room."

"So you did," said the Saint slowly.

"And then later on Mr. Devan came out of here with a man I'd never seen before. Then I thought I'd have to find out what was going on; but there was still the other man at the door—"

"What other man?"

"A sort of short thick-set man. He's been here before, with another tall man. Mr. Devan said they were salesmen. But he didn't want me to come in."

"So what did you do?" The Saint found himself curiously tense.

"Well, I didn't see why I shouldn't go into our own air-raid shelter if I wanted to. So I pretended I'd lost an earring." She had been holding her right hand a little behind her, but now she let it slip into sight. It held an ordinary household hammer. "I didn't know what I might be running into, so I brought this with me. So when he was bending down hunting around, I hit him on the head with it and came in."

The Saint couldn't laugh. That would come later . . . perhaps.

If there were any laughing afterwards.

He couldn't think of that at the instant. The simple fact and its connections backwards and forwards, and the thin incredible wisp of hope that came with them, struck into his mind with the complete breadth of a single chord. He found that he was gripping Andrea almost brutally by the shoulders.

"Where is your father now?"

"He went out with Mr. Devan and that other man. That's why I was worried, because they'd said you'd had a phone call and had to go out, but you were hoping to get back so you hadn't stopped to say goodbye to me; but I thought if you'd just passed out why should they bring you out here, and then why should they go away and leave you—"

"How long ago was this?"

She winced under the steel of his fingers, and he hardly noticed it.

"About fifteen minutes ago—"

"Show me where to find a car."

He thrust her towards the door, and flung it open, and was outside before her. He found himself in a narrow concrete corridor. At one end of it there was a flight of steps running upwards. He raced up them, and came out through an open iron door at the top, and almost tripped over the figure that lay outside.

Simon turned him over as he saved himself with one hand on the ground; and enough light came through the opening for him to recognise the chunky individual who had been Karl Morgen's companion in Washington.

He showed no signs of activity, and it seemed very possible that he had a fractured skull; but just to be on the safe side Simon gave his head another vigorous thump on the ground as he straightened himself up.

Then he was feeling his way along the paved walk that led away from the shelter, accustoming his eyes to the light of the stars and half a moon, while he heard the two girls stumbling up behind him.

Suddenly ahead of him there was a quickened heavy movement, and he had a fleeting glimpse of a tall angular silhouette against the infinitesimally lighter tint of the sky, only a scrap of a second before the beam of a flashlight stabbed at him like a spear and barely missed him as he eeled off into the shrubbery that bordered the path. The tall man came running down the wedge of his own light, not making much sound, and switched it off a moment before he came level with the Saint; and at that point Simon moved in on him without any sound at all, his left arm sliding around the man's neck from behind and locking his larynx in the crook of his elbow, cutting off voice and breath together while he spoke in the man's ear.

"You can save this for me too, bud," he said; and then he turned the man deftly around and hit him with the blade of his hand just at the base of the septum, and threw him aside into the bushes as the girls reached him.

They threaded through winding walks, down into a sunken garden and across it and out again, and then they came around a clump of trees and the house was there, looming large and sedate in the dark and seeming aloof and asleep with the heavy blackout curtains drawn. They ran around it; and on the drive in front, gleaming faintly in the dim moonlight, Simon saw Madeline Gray's car where he had parked it when he arrived.

He opened the door and she almost fell in; and then Andrea Quennel was beside him.

Her face was a pale blur in the darkness close to him.

"You must tell me," she said with a kind of blank desperation. "What is this all about?"

He was glad that she couldn't see the involuntary mask that hardened over his face. There were so many things that perhaps ought to have been said, so many things that it was impossible to say.

"I'm going to try like hell to let your father tell you himself," he said.

Then he slid in behind the wheel and slammed the door before she could ask any more, and touched the starter and whipped the car away like a racehorse from the gate, leaving her where she stood.

It was a help that he had driven himself there, and that he had a memory for landmarks and a sense of direction that a homing pigeon could have envied. In a matter of seconds he was on to the coastal road, past Compo Beach and winding along the edge of the marshes at the estuary of the Saugatuck. Then inland a little way, and then wrenching the car around to the left to speed over the bridge across the wider part of the inlet; then to the right again, northwards, to slow down a little, reluctantly, as they skimmed the edge of the town of Westport, and catch a green light and speed up again on the road that follows the west bank of the river and comes in a mile and a half to the Merritt Parkway.

They were nearly at the Parkway when Madeline said: "Wouldn't it have been better to have phoned?"

"They'd have been standing right over him when he answered the phone—if they let him answer at all. And they may be only just arriving now."

"But the police—"

He shook his head.

"With all the things I'd have to explain and convince them of, and then to get them moving fast enough? No. It's the same as our trip from Washington. Only worse. But this time perhaps we won't be too late."

She sat tense and still, leaning forward a little, as if by that she could help the car to make more speed.

"Have we any chance?"

"We're trying."

And they were on the Parkway, the speedometer needle climbing to eighty and eighty-five and creeping on, yet with the Saint's fingers effortless and almost caressing on the wheel, driving with one hand only while the other pressed the electric lighter and shook a cigarette out of Devan's pack and set it between his lips.

Presently she said, as if because any kind of conversation was better than listening to the same ceaseless clock-tick of terror: "How much does Andrea know?"

"I think she's fairly dumb," he said in the same way. "Devan said she was dumb. They just used her. And so did I. As I told you, in Washington I eventually tried to let her think she'd taken me in, because she might be a useful contact. And she was."

"But now you know why she asked you over there tonight."

"I know why she asked me in the first place. They had a story for her, and they must have known from past experience that she shouldn't be hard to sell. Maybe she never has been quite so monumentally dumb, but she knew how to leave her brain alone. It was the easiest defence of her own kind of Social Stability . . . Only, as it worked out this evening, I invited myself."

"And she let you walk into it."

"She knew that I knew what I was walking into. She tried to stop me last night, when I didn't know. She may have figured that I had all the right cards

up my sleeve, or else I wouldn't want to walk in.
She may have changed sides again, and been glad
to see me sticking my neck out. It might have been
vengeance, or it might have been her kind of help;
or she might have just put her brain to sleep again.
I wouldn't know. She must have done a lot of odd
things in her life that you couldn't explain in ten-
year-old language."

"Only she fell in love with you," Madeline said.
"I've heard all your story, and I've seen her."

The Saint let cigarette smoke trail away from his
lips, and kept his eyes on the unfolding road.

"I didn't make her do that." He was cold and
apart in a way that she had never felt from him
before. "She saved our lives tonight, whether she
knew it or not, and whatever she meant to do. Don't
ever forget that." There were some things that it
was almost impossible to put together in words.
"I'm afraid nothing is going to be easy for her
now."

And they were past Talmadge Hill, swooping
down and up long easy switchbacks, the engine
humming to the perfection of its power, the tires
hissing on the roadbed and the wind ruffling at the
windows, almost as if they were flying, the sense of
speed lulled by the smoothness of his driving and
the isolation of the darkness around them, with only
the road to see ahead and the tail lights of other cars
being overtaken like crawling glowworms and flut-
tering angrily for an instant as they were passed and
then being lost in silence behind.

He thought, this was one time when he didn't
give a damn if the whole Highway Patrol was out
after him, and just because of that there wouldn't
be a single one of them in the country. And there
wasn't.

And then they were near the turning he had to take, and suddenly he recognised it, and crammed on the brakes and spun the wheel and spurred the engine, and they were screaming around and bucking through a break in the highway division, right under the lights of some inoffensive voyager in the other lane who probably lost two pounds of weight and a year's growth on the spot, while the Saint balanced the car against its own rolling momentum like a tightrope walker and dived it into the twisting lane that led towards Calvin Gray's home.

It was only then that she said: "Have you got a gun or anything?"

"I borrowed one from Karl. He owed me something," he said, and didn't bother to explain about Karl.

And then they were nearing the entrance of Gray's estate, and he killed the engine and cut the lights and coasted the car to a stop a few yards short of the stone gateway.

He got out and said "This way," and drew her out through the same door, and closed it again without a sound, and they went quickly in up the drive and past the house, as softly as he could lead her. There was a great silence all around them now, with even the undertones of their own traveling wiped out, and he realised that for miles his ears had been keyed for the sound that he dreaded and that he must have heard, the concussion of unnatural thunder and the blaze of unnatural lightning that would have said finally that they were too late. And it still might come at any instant, but so far it hadn't, and the only light was the faint untroubled silver of the moon.

He only took her so far because he wanted to be sure that he found the right path; and then they found it, and he knew exactly where he was, and he stopped for a second to halt her.

"You wait here. Lie down, and be quiet."

"I want to go with you."

"You couldn't do anything. And you'd make more noise than I will. And if anything happens, somebody has to tell the story."

His lips touched her face, and he was gone, and he had scarcely paused at all.

And so perhaps this was the end of all stories; and if it was, there could have been worse ones.

He came like a shadow to the door of the laboratory building, and turned the handle without a sound with his left hand while his right slid the borrowed revolver out of his pocket. His nerves were spidery threads of ice, and time stood still around him like a universe that had run down.

He thought then, in a crazy disassociation, that it would be strange to die that way, because you would never even know you died. You wouldn't even have time to hear or feel anything. There would be some sort of silent and insensate shock that would take the inside of your mind and blot it out, like the putting out of a light and a great hand that picked you up and wiped you away. One instant you would be there, and the next instant you wouldn't be there, but it wouldn't mean anything, because you wouldn't be there to know.

Through the tiny hall, as he went in, he could see all of them by the long bench where the rubber apparatus was set up. He could see Hobart Quennel, balanced and absorbed in watching, and Walter Devan standing a little back with one hand in the side pocket of his coat, and Calvin Gray's thin hands adjusting themselves around a large glass flask of strawcolored liquid to pick it up.

The Saint stood in the doorway with his gun leveled, and tried to launch his voice on the air like a feather, mostly so that it would steal into the ears of Calvin Gray without any shock that might precipitate disaster.

"I'm sorry, boys," he said, "but this is the end of the line. Please keep still and put your hands up very slowly."

He saw Quennel and Devan start to turn towards him, and then begin to obey when they saw what he held in his hand. But he was really hardly noticing them at all. His eyes were on Calvin Gray; and he felt as though he had stopped breathing a long time ago.

It was a slightly cosmic thing that he had reckoned without the scientific temperament and the contempt of familiarity.

Calvin Gray settled the flask back on the table as if it had been a soft-shelled egg, and dusted off his hands.

"I'm glad you didn't startle me," he said. "That thing is full of nitroglycerin, and I was just going to drop it."

7

How Simon Templar went on his Way.

Jetterick, the FBI man, tried to straighten a limp
cigarette and said: "One thing that puzzles me is
how Gray could put a bowl of soup like that together with Quennel watching him. If Quennel was a
chemist himself once—"

"So far as I know," said the Saint, "he only
worked in a drug store. He got out of the racket
very soon to be a business man. And there were a lot
of unlabeled bottles in the laboratory—I'd noticed
that before. Gray, and his daughter knew what they
were, but nobody else did. And one solution looks
like a lot of others, at a glance. And Quennel was
just interested in what he was being told . . . Anyhow, it doesn't matter a lot now. It didn't quite
come to that."

"What about Quennel's daughter?" Jetterick
asked.

Simon Templar looked out of the window into
the dark.

"See what her story is, and I'll confirm it where I
can." His voice was scrupulously commonplace—
perhaps too scrupulously. "You can say that she
must have been in a tough spot, trying to be loyal to

her father and at the same time trying to follow . . . some other influences. But she did try in her way to keep me out of that Imberline setup. I don't think you can make her an accessory to that. I don't think she ever knew that Imberline was booked for the big voyage. Probably Quennel and Devan didn't even know it then. But she overheard just enough, and she'd assimilated enough general background, to be sure that the Savoy Plaza could be an unhealthy joint for me to go home to . . . And she did let us out tonight—otherwise none of us would be talking now . . . You'll do what the book tells you; but I'd like to see her come out as well as she can."

And he remembered her lips and her eyes and her white shoulders, and all of her asking impossible things.

Jetterick's taciturn stare took its time over him. "If your evidence holds up, it'll be quite a case."

"It'll hold up. And it will be quite a case. Quennel got to be a damn brilliant lawyer in his day, but he'll have to be more than brilliant to laugh this one off . . . I'm glad it was this way instead of the other, for more reasons than one. A little fresh air on the subject won't do any harm at all." The Saint stood up. "I'll go back to New Haven with you and help you fill in the picture. And somewhere along the line I've got to call a guy named Hamilton, who's going to be sore as a hangnail if he has to get this story out of his morning paper."

"Come over any time tomorrow," said Jetterick accommodatingly. "You've been through a hell of a lot, and I guess you could do with a rest."

"Let's do it tonight," said the Saint quietly.

He emptied an ashtray into the fireplace, and settled his coat; and it was as if everything began again.

He said: "There's still a war going on, and I don't know enough about tomorrow."

He went out and found Calvin Gray, and said goodnight to him; but Madeline followed him out to the car.

"You will be coming back, won't you?" she said.

"Very soon, I hope."

He had so many meanings in his mind that he couldn't help which one she chose from his voice. He sat beside the FBI man and gazed steadily ahead as the lane swam tortuously at them and swallowed them again. He wanted to believe that he might be going back there some day. There was no harm in hoping.

HEALTH AND BEAUTY—ADVICE FROM THE EXPERTS